THE MICE MAN COMETH

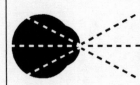

This Large Print Book carries the
Seal of Approval of N.A.V.H.

NOSY IN NEBRASKA, BOOK 3

THE MICE MAN COMETH

A MAXIE THE MOUSE MYSTERY

MARY CONNEALY

THORNDIKE PRESS
A part of Gale, Cengage Learning

GALE
CENGAGE Learning

Detroit • New York • San Francisco • New Haven, Conn • Waterville, Maine • London

GALE
CENGAGE Learning

LIBRARY OF CONGRESS CATALOGING-IN-PUBLICATION DATA

Connealy, Mary.
  The mice man cometh / by Mary Connealy.
    p. cm. — (Nosy in Nebraska ; bk. 3) (Thorndike Press large
print Christian mystery)
  "A Maxie the Mouse Mystery."
  ISBN-13: 978-1-4104-3652-8 (hardcover)
  ISBN-10: 1-4104-3652-7 (hardcover)
  1. Large type books. I. Title.
PS3603.O544M53 2011
813'.6—dc22   2011009944

Published in 2011 by arrangement with Barbour Publishing, Inc.

Printed in Mexico
1 2 3 4 5 6 7 15 14 13 12 11

My mom, Dorothy Moore, would jump and squeal when she saw a mouse — but she wasn't so afraid that she wouldn't go after them with a broom. I'm not sure why I ended up being more of a coward than her. A sad commentary on how Americans are getting soft, I suppose . . .

My mother-in-law, Marybelle Connealy is completely unafraid. I saw her empty a mouse trap of its ghastly contents once. She dropped the horrid carcass out of the trap, and picked the mouse up by its long, repugnant tail. I squeaked and jumped, and she rolled her eyes at me, saying, "It won't hurt you, honey."

1

Tyler Simpson pounded his head with his fist, hoping his brain would start up.

Think, think, think. He knew the boys were behaving terribly, but he didn't know what to say or do to stop them. He struggled with every decision as if he still needed his wife to dictate every move he made.

Being dead was a huge stumbling block to her being in charge. Not insurmountable, though. He could still hear her nagging in his head. It had been burned into his brain.

Benetton roared into the room, his arms spread wide, pretending to be a plane. Skidding into a box of breakables. Tyler upgraded his son from plane to dive-bomber. Benetton sprinted up the open stairway to the second floor of the new law office.

In Melnik.

Tyler Simpson's law office.

There's one decision he'd made.

Liza had to be spinning in her grave.

7

In addition to operating a private practice, Tyler was the new attorney for the city of Melnik, and he had been appointed county attorney to fill a vacancy.

That screamed conflict of interest.

What if the city and county had a legal dispute? No one but Tyler seemed to care, and since the city and county were in complete agreement with the first case coming to trial — as was Tyler, who wanted to crush the defendant like a slimy cockroach — he'd signed on.

Melvin Melnik had tried to kill Bonnie, Tyler's sister.

Tyler's younger son raced up the stairs, and Tyler followed. Who knew whether the second floor was safe? He saw Giancarlo's blond head disappear. Tyler was as blond as most Swedes, and his boys had taken after him.

He reached the upstairs and looked to the right, past a door to the building that shared a wall with his, past a ceiling-high cupboard, and out to a window overlooking Main Street. To his left he saw a mountain of dust-covered boxes of junk. The walls were lined with tall oak cabinets, painted seasick green, most with doors sagging on their hinges.

The door to his right opened, slamming

into his face.

He sprawled backward, landing with a crash, the pain blinding him. A cloud of dust kicked up when he hit, nearly choking him. All he could think of were the stairs.

He clawed at the floor. Fear of plunging down the steps he'd just ascended overrode the pain. He stopped skidding. His head dangled over the steep drop. The ringing in his ears eased enough that he heard the boys still shouting and running as he scooted on his back to solid ground. His eyes blinked open.

Lying there, ground into the dirt, in agony, his brain blurry, he saw . . . the prettiest woman who ever lived. Leaning over him. Her eyes wide with worry about him. She cared about him.

"I'm so sorry." She . . . lilted. Her voice was accented, British. "I say, are you all right, sir?" She dropped to her knees and blinked concerned eyes, almost lost under a pair of glasses with small rectangular black frames. Black hair pulled back at her nape. Creamy white skin with rosy cheeks, blue eyes that seemed to sing . . . or maybe he'd just been hit so hard that little birds were flying around his head tweeting. He'd been assaulted by a bespectacled Snow White.

His eyes focused on . . . pencils . . . stuck

in her hair. Too many to count. The blow to his head must have been harder than he'd thought.

Her hands went to his face, and a long ponytail rained over her shoulder. She brushed soft fingers over his cheeks, a furrow between her blue eyes.

"Sir, sir, answer me, please." She dropped her *r*'s. It was cultured. Like Princess Diana. Or Princess Snow White.

Please, Lord, don't cast me as a dwarf.

"Shall I summon a physician?" That voice — she might have been singing. Or casting a spell.

Fairy tales, princesses, magic . . . he tried to think. "I'm . . . I'm okay." His jaw worked under protest. "No permanent damage."

He wasn't absolutely sure about that. His nose throbbed like a sore tooth; his forehead did, too. As a matter of fact, his teeth throbbed like sore teeth. And the worst damage was that he didn't want her to quit touching him. He might not recover from that.

She leaned back, still kneeling. Still pencil-adorned. "So sorry about that. I didn't know anyone was about until I heard the ruckus." She pointed with one thumb over her shoulder at his rampaging sons. "I'm letting the flat next over, the whole building

10

actually." She pointed at the door she'd nailed him with, which had to be an entrance to the old opera house, abandoned for even longer than Tyler's building.

"You live in Melnik?" He had to ask. Two and two were not adding up to four. Why would a magical fairy princess move to Melnik? Maybe she was under a spell and had been cast out of her palace and into — Nebraska.

She didn't answer. "I'd barely noticed that door. I heard voices." Sliding an arm around his back, she leaned so close her silken hair brushed across his neck.

What was she doing?

He shivered. His breath caught. His heart hammered.

And how could he help her do it?

"Come, my good man, let's get you up." She lifted.

He figured it out, jumped to his feet, and sent her staggering into the edge of the open door. She banged her head and rubbed it, but didn't cry out or scold him. In fact, except for the rubbing, she acted as if a blow to the head were nothing.

Tyler could relate.

He reached for her. "I'm sorry. I didn't mean to hurt you."

Ducking away, she smiled. "We're even,

11

then. Well, ta-ta." She turned to leave in a whirl of clothing. Now that he saw all of her, he realized she wore a ridiculous outfit, including khaki pants that came almost to her armpits. A white blouse, tucked in but so baggy it could have come out of Tyler's closet, and he was at least five inches taller than her, although she was tall, five-seven maybe. She was filthy. Most likely her building matched his for dust. The mannish clothes swallowed her whole but did nothing to conceal how lovely she was. Not even the pencils detracted. They only made him curious.

Out the corner of his eye, Tyler caught something whizzing toward his head. He ducked. The object shattered against the wall. He was grateful for the distraction, because he hadn't thought of a woman — as a woman — since Liza died. Honestly, it had been long before that, because he hadn't seen anything attractive about Liza for most of their marriage.

What had he been thinking to marry so young, have children so young?

"What are you thinking, to let your boys destroy these artifacts?" She hadn't minded getting knocked into an oak door, but now the woman glared at the broken object with intelligent, cranky eyes. His attraction died

12

a sudden and complete death. He was done with cranky women.

Done with all women.

Tyler realized he'd been standing still too long.

Thirty years too long, but that was another story.

"Boys, come here, please."

They kept running and shouting. There was another crash.

"I've a surprise for you, lads." The woman's crisp, accented voice drew them. It drew him, too.

She was the Pied Piper.

Her voice was a flute.

He was the King of Rats.

The boys raced over, Benetton hopping from foot to foot. Giancarlo, filthy even for a kid playing in a room coated with dirt, ricocheted into the tall cupboard beside the open door to Snow White's building. The cupboard door cracked. Mercifully, it was made of solid oak, so it held — barely.

"What are your names, lads?"

Tyler hoped she'd keep talking. He was enchanted by that Pied Piper voice.

Benetton must not have liked it as well. He shrieked in her face. A roar, bared teeth — it reminded Tyler of a movie he'd watched about a woman who lived in Africa

13

with a herd of gorillas.

And if his new neighbor was Jane Good-
all, that made his son an ape.

Giancarlo reached for the pocket of her
clown pants. He must have thought the
surprise was there and he had a right to it.
Her pants dropped from her armpits to her
hips, and she tugged them back up.

Giancarlo searched. She stared at him in
apparent fascination. The boy came up
empty-handed. Benetton screamed again.

"Where is it?" Giancarlo, rude as his big
brother, Benetton, was a bit quieter and
more dangerous. "Where's our surprise?"

Little Brother Syndrome, Liza had called
it, as if labeling it made it okay for the boy
to be such a brat.

Snow White had a pencil behind her ear,
besides the ones in her hair. She grabbed it
and tugged a small spiral-bound notebook
from the breast pocket of her blouse. She
dropped the notebook, bent to get it, and
cracked heads with Giancarlo. The boy staggered back, shrieking in pain. He crashed
into the cupboard again. It tilted ominously,
and Tyler watched it, coiled to dive for his
son and drag him to safety. The cupboard
stayed upright.

"Oops, so sorry." Snow White said it like a
knee-jerk reaction. Tyler wondered how

14

many people she'd knocked into in her life. He'd met her about two minutes ago and she'd already gotten him and Giancarlo. He resisted the temptation to push Benetton behind his back.

Retrieving the notebook while Giancarlo screamed in mock agony, Snow White tore off her glasses, thrust them into her breast pocket, and started jotting. Leaning close to her paper, she worked in rapt concentration. She flipped to a new page and hurried on with her writing.

Within seconds, she tore the pages out of her notebook and handed one to each boy. Giancarlo was interested enough to quit screaming.

Tyler was beside Giancarlo, so he saw it. A drawing. A caricature of his son, looking a bit too real. Benetton's mouth open, his teeth gaping. Fanglike, but there was no mistaking that it was Benetton.

Giancarlo looked like a pig, his nose a little snouty, but the grime was a true depiction.

The boys laughed.

"Draw one of Dad," Benetton yelled.

Giancarlo took up the chorus.

She glanced at Tyler for no more than three seconds, then drew. His took longer. The boys stood still the whole time. A first.

She tore the page off and stuck the pencil back in her hair, missing her ear. He suspected she'd never find it. He looked at the picture.

Grief and loneliness.

It wasn't true.

He hadn't grieved for his wife, and he wanted to be alone. The boys pulled on his arms and snatched the picture away, hooting and making jokes about how dumb he looked.

That was nothing compared to how enraged he felt.

It took all his willpower not to snatch the paper back and rip it in half. Furious — irrationally furious — his cheeks heated and his temper roared. He kept it all inside. Liza had made him an expert at self-control.

The woman turned away without realizing she'd just detonated a bomb and said to the boys, "I'm Dr. Stuart. How do you lads feel about Maxie the Mouse?"

"Max-ee, Max-ee, Max-ee!" Benetton chanted like a cheerleader whipping up team spirit.

"We love him!" Giancarlo grabbed her baggy pants and used her for balance as he jumped up and down. He smeared her already-filthy clothes with more dirt. Her pants sagged. Tyler thought they were going

16

all the way to her ankles. But the belt held low on her hips.

Tyler felt a whoosh of relief; then a second later, he realized he was staring at those hips. He tore his eyes away. It was so hard, he could almost hear the tearing sound.

"Excellent. You young lads want to come over and see my flat? Lots to destroy over there."

"What's a flat?" Benetton shoved past her.

"It's an apartment. *Flat* is an English term."

"We speak English and we've never heard of it." Benetton whirled toward the door. A new world to conquer.

Dr. Snow White scratched her forehead. A red welt had appeared where she'd cracked heads with Giancarlo, and now the bump had dirty fingerprints on it. "I'm going to be living in the upstairs and working down-stairs."

With shouts of joy, they leapt toward her . . . flat? They bounced off him and the messy doctor and the oak cupboard then charged through the door and were gone.

"Wait, they can't —"

"They're going to make a great case study." Her eyes glowed with fervor usually reserved for Dr. Frankenstein during a lightning storm. She turned and followed

17

the boys, snapping the door shut in his face.

"Case study?" Tyler spoke to an empty, dust-choked room. He reached for the knob. His first thought was Stranger Danger. But in this case, the stranger was in more danger than his boys.

Something — a body — thudded against the wall, right next to the door. Was it Dr. Snow White or one of his sons? His sons bounced without breaking their bones, but the doctor might be more fragile.

A thud came again, this one right beside that tippy cupboard, and Tyler heard something crack. The cupboard had two doors, floor to ceiling. One of them swung open an inch, but they were latched and padlocked and the lock held.

Dr. Snow White emerged from her kidnapping and shut the door behind her. "You mind if I step back in here until they've finished exploring?"

Exploring struck him as a very polite word for it.

"What are your sons' names?"

"Benetton and Giancarlo."

Her dark brows arched above the glasses she'd put back on. "Their names are Benetton and Giancarlo?"

Tyler felt his cheeks flush. "Yes."

"So . . ." She studied his dark blond hair

18

for a bit. "You're Italian?"

"My wife was."

"Was?"

"Yes."

"I did two years of anthropological under-grad studies in Italy. Perhaps I researched her family. What was her maiden name?"

"Barnston."

She turned and frowned at him. "Excuse me? Italian?"

"On her mother's side . . . back a ways . . . like five generations."

"And yet she gave her sons Italian names? I say, how odd."

Tyler decided it was his turn. "Case study?"

Another crash echoed through the adjoining wall. Her smile, vague and lovely, re-appeared. She seemed to be in complete accord with him. As if she'd read his mind, knew the boys were dangerous, and had come back in here to save herself.

He should have been insulted. Instead, his respect for her blossomed, and he caught himself staring again. Her skin was flawless. Filthy, but flawless. It was milky white, and those rosebud cheeks, even smudged with dirt, were impossibly beautiful.

"Yes, didn't I mention I'm here in Melnik to study —"

Another crash interrupted her. The single thin wall — all that separated him from this lovely, lovely woman — vibrated.

The cupboard cracked again and the padlock popped off.

The door blasted open, pushed by the weight of . . .

Melvin Melnik's . . .

Dead . . .

Body.

2

Maddy Stuart jumped and squeaked, colliding with her neighbor.

The corpse landed on a box directly in front of the cupboard and cartwheeled over it, smashing his legs out the window before he quit rolling.

Tyler's strong arms went around her for just a second, one surprisingly pleasant second.

Shocking how pleasant.

Considering the corpse, pleasant should have been beyond her. Then the father with the sad brown eyes and a pillaging horde for children surged past her and knelt by the obviously, utterly, indisputably dead man.

He pressed two fingers to the man's throat then looked over his shoulder. "Call 911."

Excellent; she needed an excuse to run.

A resounding crash in her flat stopped her from reaching for her own door. No reason to go in there, anyway. "I don't have a telephone. My mobile unit doesn't work here, I've discovered." It might have quit working altogether since she hadn't paid the bill for two months.

"There's one on my desk downstairs."

Glad to leave the corpse, Maddy hesitated for a second. "What's the number?"

The new neighbor looked up. "For 911?"

"Yes."

His head tilted as if his brain didn't work on the level. "It's . . . uh . . . 9-1-1."

"Oh, well, that explains why you Americans call it that." She turned and ran, reaching the ground level without mishap. Refreshing, that. Stairs were her nemesis.

It took a matter of seconds to reach the dispatcher, and before she was done talking, she heard a siren go off in what sounded like the next building. Why hadn't he just told her to run next door? What an odd little village.

She turned her thoughts away from the man . . . men . . . upstairs. The living one almost as interesting as the dead. Well, more interesting actually; after all, he was alive. Of course, the dead one was dead, and that was extremely interesting — in a horrifying kind of way.

The man — the live one — called down,

"Can you come up here and occupy the boys so they don't walk in on this?"

The rabble he called sons would most likely adore seeing a corpse. She was delighted to run across these lads, who were entranced even at their young age by the mighty rodent this village seemed to worship.

What an opportunity!

She hoped to enhance her résumé enough to be considered for a full professorship at Oxford by the time she was done with Melnik and Maxie the Mouse. Those boys were a good place to start.

The police car pulled up before she could return to watch the boys. She let a man in who was uniformed and balding. She saw the notebook in his breast pocket and liked him immediately.

"You found a dead body?"

"Yes, Officer, follow me. The deceased is upstairs."

The man lumbered behind her. "I don't s'pose there's a chance on earth he died of natural causes?"

Madeline tripped on the first stair and fell forward, catching herself and hardly missing a step. She tugged up her pants, wondering why they wouldn't stay at her waist, and looked back as she walked. "I suppose it's

23

possible he did, though I doubt he stuffed himself into that cupboard, and it's even less likely that he padlocked the door from the outside after himself."

The older man's shoulders slumped. Madeline heard him mutter, "There is no crime in Melnik. There is no crime in Melnik. There is no crime in Melnik."

Add a pair of ruby slippers clicked together, and perhaps a Good Witch of the North, and who knows where the man might end up. Madeline reached the top of the stairs, saw the gaping eyes of the departed, and doubted any amount of wishing would erase this crime from Melnik.

Her neighbor, crouching by the side of the corpse, looked up. "Okay, good. I can watch the boys now."

Madeline shivered from her proximity to the cadaver. "I'll help."

"I'll need to talk to you, Ty. And Melnik's gonna need a prosecutor on this."

Tie? What kind of odd name was that? Benetton? Giancarlo? She'd assumed Swedish from their name and coloring. So if his Swedish sons were named after Italians, perhaps he was named after an ascot.

Americans. Such an odd lot.

"No kidding." Tie rose to his feet and stepped back. "I checked for a pulse even

24

though it was obviously too late. Other than that, I didn't touch a thing. He fell out of that cupboard." Her neighbor pointed. "We both saw the padlock pop off."

"We?" the constable asked.

"She and I." Tyler nodded in Madeline's direction.

"I'm Dr. Madeline Stuart," Madeline said to the hefty officer of the law.

"Yeah, I know."

"How could you know? I've only been in town two hours, and I haven't spoken to anyone except" — she couldn't say "Tie," too odd — "him and his sons."

Glass shattered in the next room. The father with the sad eyes, who referred to his wife by saying "was," dove for the door and rushed in.

Madeline followed.

"Miss?"

She turned back to the constable.

"We heard someone had rented that building from Joe Manning, but no one knows what for."

"It's no secret." It was a secret. If the town knew the whole truth, any information would be tainted. But the basic information she was willing to share. "I'm an anthropologist."

"An . . . an . . . what?"

25

"I'm studying small-town life in America. Your charming village came to my attention because of the news stories about your Melnik Historical Society and your world-famous mouse. I'm here to write my doctoral thesis."

"Don't antheologists dig up Egyptian tombs?"

"That's archaeologists. I'm an anthropologist, completely different, I assure you. I'll do no digging. I promise not to get underfoot. We can surely talk more after you've . . ." She jerked her head at the corpse.

"Oh, sure. What's your name again?"

Weren't lawmen supposed to listen to details? She'd already said her name. A bloodcurdling scream sounded from her flat. She had next to nothing in there as of yet, but she'd soon need sturdy furniture if those boys were going to be regular visitors. And since she'd just decided to center her case study around them, they most likely would be dropping by.

She extended her fingers, intending to shake hands, and managed to smack her knuckles on the constable's enormous silver belt buckle. Withdrawing and taking better aim, she managed to connect with his hand this time. "Dr. Madeline Stuart. I'm planning to live on the upper floor of the building those boys are right now dismantling brick by brick, so you can reach me easily enough."

The man nodded. "I'm Sheriff Hammerstad."

The downstairs door crashed open. Refreshing, that — to have something crashing around in someone else's building.

"He's dead?" The cry, euphoric, shook dust loose from overhead. It drifted down on Madeline, Constable Hammerstad, and the dead man. Madeline couldn't get any dirtier, and the dead man was beyond caring. The constable, though, seemed annoyed as he swiped at his gray uniform.

Madeline decided that the boys had learned their manners from others in town.

"The man who tried to steal Maxie Mouse from this town is dead? Hallelujah!" A vision in primary colors appeared at the bottom of the steps. A turbaned woman, rotund, swathed in a caftan that looked like Technicolor fairies had splashed her with their wands, charged upstairs.

"Tallulah, stay down there. This is a crime scene."

Tallulah? Madeline had made note of a woman named Tallulah. She'd planned to interview the woman. With her outrageous

27

name — the town seemed to be rife with them — Maddy decided this had to be her. And the woman's mention of Maxie the Mouse was as good as a signed, notarized confirmation.

By the time the constable had quit scolding Tallulah to stay away, she stood at his side. Presumably, since she hadn't quit prattling the whole time she climbed the stairs, she hadn't heard the constable's order. Maddy noticed an odd-looking purse in the woman's hand. It looked rather like a birdcage, only not domed. A lovely, wired, rectangular shape. Before Maddy could figure out what it was, another woman appeared, slower, but fast enough for someone who appeared to be eighty.

"Dora, not you, too? Both of you, get out of here." The officer waved his arm, shooing Tallulah and Dora like they were a flock of chickens.

Dora looked at the corpse, then at Madeline. Her dust mop of gray hair quivered as if she couldn't decide who was more interesting. Madeline felt pinned by the beady, inquiring eyes and hoped the woman chose the corpse.

Tie poked his head through the door. He looked straight at her, and she forgot all about Melnik.

Those sad eyes.

His wife had certainly died. He needed comfort. He needed compassion. He needed gentle touches. He needed . . .

"I need you."

"You do?" How lovely.

"Yeah, my boys may have destroyed something valuable. You'd better come and check."

He needed a whip and chair.

Since she didn't have anything valuable except her computer, which was still in the boot of her car, Madeline wasn't concerned. But Tie had told her to come. She feared she'd follow him anywhere.

She didn't ask for permission; she just left the dead body she'd helped discover, barely noticing several more people trooping up the stairs while the constable scolded them all.

Her upstairs was mostly empty, unlike Tie's, which was piled with dust-covered boxes. She experienced a pang of jealousy for all those boxes Tie got to sift through. She'd have loved to be in possession of all those artifacts. She'd carried up a few boxes of clothing. Unbreakable, but strewn about now, thanks to the boys.

She knew little about the town except what she'd read in the paper, but she knew anthropology. She knew every town had its roots, its eccentricities. Any small village made a good case study. But she hoped to find something more here. Something enduring and valuable that would be printed again and again in textbooks — each paying substantial royalties.

A small, isolated civilization within America that had evolved into something completely unique due to the people's adoration of a giant rodent. She'd already named it.

Maxie Madness.

Catchy.

Not just a dusty thesis, bound and buried in a college library. A book, a *New York Times* best seller. She might be British, but she could smell the interview on *Oprah*.

She followed Tie's broad shoulders and the noise to her lower level. She'd left a few things when she'd come to town last week. She'd spent the winter in Omaha, teaching and researching for her thesis. She'd planned to write the paper on the unique psychology of a small American village. That's when she'd found Melnik.

Her neighbor had found a broom.

He swept glass shards while the boys rummaged. She suspected Tie spent most of his life doing exactly this same thing.

She stared at his sons, her mind given to thinking in caricatures. Hyperactive ferrets came to mind. Her front door opened and a very pregnant woman wearing a bright red dress, obviously maternity, strolled in.

"Ben! Johnny!" One clap of the hands, and the boys were right in front of her, quiet, attentive. Madeline marveled.

A tall, good-looking man followed her, watching her closely. Apparently his only duty in life was to make sure this woman didn't stumble and take a fall.

"Do you boys want to go swimming?"

Screams of joy erupted from the lads.

"Then we can go for ice cream. Jansson's has chocolate today."

The boys jumped up and down. The pregnant woman clapped those magic hands. "The ice cream is off if you get rowdy."

The jumping stopped. They chorused, "Yes, Aunt Bonnie, we'll be good. Hi, Uncle Joe."

"Hi, boys." The man smiled at the children as if he took pure delight in them. Something Maddy hadn't seen from their father. All things considered, Maddy decided Tie's reactions made more sense.

The kindly man looked at her and waved. "Hello, Dr. Stuart. Hope you're finding everything here to suit you."

"It's fine. Thanks." Though why this man should care, she had no idea.

"I'm Joe. You rented the building from me."

Oh, well, that explained how he knew her. They'd done their business over the phone and through the mail. He'd even sent the front door key in a parcel.

Maddy, being a scientist and of an analytical nature, studied the extraordinary effect of the chap on the two boys. She pondered his facial expression, not discounting the bribery, and planned to duplicate it.

She extracted her memo pad from her blouse pocket, hunted for a pencil behind her ear, and found none. She was forever misplacing pencils. She grabbed one the boys had knocked off her battered metal desk and made a note.

"Go on ahead, then." Bonnie shooed the boys out. "Your swimsuits are in my car out front."

"I'll walk with them to the pool, honey. You can drive down or go home and rest."

Bonnie smiled, so delighted you'd think the man had just discovered sliced bread. He leaned down and gave her a quick kiss, resting one hand on her stomach, his eyes glowing.

His gesture made something hard clog Maddy's throat. No man had ever, in her long, clumsy life, looked at her that way.

"I'm going to take a nap. If you're not home when I wake up, I'll drive down to the pool and give you all a ride home. See you later, Tyler."

Tyler, not Tie. It made sense now. And Bonnie was certainly a respectable name. Also, it was another name that had come up in Maddy's research.

The boys raced out, quiet now, but no less energetic. Through her huge front windows, Maddy saw them swinging open the doors of a red Jeep.

Tyler looked up from his broom, scowling. "I've told you not to call them Ben and Johnny."

The newcomer had been turning to leave, but she stopped and laughed in the grouchy man's surly face. "Yeah, keep at me. I'm sure I'll remember one of these days." Aunt Bonnie adjusted a red headband that perfectly matched her dress as she came farther into the room to give Tyler a hug. She turned quiet, intelligent eyes on Madeline.

Maddy saw the resemblance between Bonnie and Tyler. Add the huge "Aunt Bonnie" clue from Tyler's sons, and Maddy deduced that these two were brother and sister. Really, was what Sherlock Holmes did such a big trick?

"Hello. You're Madeline Stuart, then. Joe, my husband, who just ran out of here, didn't introduce me. I'm Bonnie Manning, Tyler's *biiiig* sister." She patted her rounded tummy and laughed. "Welcome to Melnik. I work in the building on the other side of Ty. I'm the curator of the Melnik Historical Society Museum."

Yes. Bonnie Manning! Her day was off to a smashing start. Well, except for the corpse. Maddy had stumbled onto the very person she'd hoped to work with most closely. And Bonnie was the boys' aunt. Perfect.

"I hope Ben and Johnny didn't wreck your stuff."

"No, nothing of any value."

"Bonnie, those nicknames —"

Bonnie turned back to Tyler. "You hear yourself, right? That's coming straight out of Liza's mouth, not yours, Ty."

"I just think we should —"

"Hush." Bonnie hugged him again, not that easy with her extended middle. "I heard about Melvin; that's why I came to get the boys. Joe can watch them at the pool; then they can come over to the building site."

"How's the new museum coming?" Tyler asked.

"Great. We should be ready to move in by the end of summer, I hope. So I suppose Cousin Junior will want to ask you some questions."

Cousin Junior?

Tyler nodded and took a step back. "Sure, I suppose. Melvin died in my building. But I don't know much."

"Well, the important thing is, he's dead." Bonnie ran a loving hand over her enormous belly, seeming quite chipper, considering her bloodthirsty pronouncement. "He can't haunt anyone anymore and he can't take Maxie."

Madeline felt her ears perk up at another mention of the mouse. Maxie had already come up several times. Excellent. There was a good chance these people were as crazy as she suspected.

Tyler clasped Bonnie's hand. "I was scared for you and Joe. I had hoped to convince a judge to revoke Melvin's bail, but now there's no need."

So Tyler had actually been more concerned with human beings than the mouse. Madeline discarded him as a possible subject, but Bonnie was still at the top of the list, as well as Tyler's boys.

Bonnie nodded at Madeline as she turned toward the door. "Nice to meet you."

Madeline hurried forward. "It's Dr. Madeline Stuart, and I'm here in town to study the history of Melnik, and that, of course, includes Maxie, the World's Largest Field Mouse. The Historical Society Museum will most assuredly be a vital resource for my work. And I'd love a chance to visit with you, too."

Bonnie nodded. "That's great. Maxie has brought this town back to life. He's the hero of Melnik."

Tyler snorted.

Madeline shoved him even further off her list.

"He's a symbol of everything great about Melnik. I'm always happy to talk about him."

Bonnie smiled and waddled out of the building, one hand resting on the small of her back.

Madeline was exuberant. She'd only been in town one day and she'd already befriended, in a nonsuspicious way, one of the most strident Maxie worshippers. Bonnie's name had figured prominently in many of the papers she'd read, along with Tallulah, the colorful, turbaned woman from upstairs, and a newspaper editor named Carrie O'Connor. Two down, one to go.

She reached behind her ear, realized she'd

lost her pencil again, and found one on her desk. Retrieving her notebook from her pocket, she began jotting.

"What made you draw that picture of me?"

Madeline had forgotten Tyler was there. She looked up. Into the saddest eyes she'd ever seen. "I draw what I see."

His eyes flashed, anger over top of the grief. "And you see sadness when you look at me?"

Madeline's heart turned over with compassion. Not only sadness but denial. A classic case of arrested grief. He must have loved his wife very much. And of course he would. A young man like this, with two beautiful boys who were obviously showing signs of rebellion, no doubt based on their own grief. A tragedy.

"Did you see sadness when I showed you that picture?"

"You drew it. You put it there. You heard about my wife dying and projected that onto me."

Madeline wasn't sure how to proceed. Her specialty was the study of civilizations. She was quite proficient with papers and artifacts, but actual human beings were beyond her. Rather a fatal flaw in an anthropologist. That's why this Melnik paper was so crucial. A well-done thesis that turned into a well-received book could make her faltering career.

"I didn't mean to hurt your feelings. I won't be drawing any more pictures of you. I promise."

"That's not the point." He pulled the picture out of his back pocket. He'd folded it. Obviously not planning to cherish her work of high art.

He stuck it in her face. "The point is, you are a very talented caricaturist."

Maddy marveled at his use of the big word. She hadn't expected much of an intellectual bent in a small mid-American town.

"That gives you the power to hurt. You gave my sons insulting animal characteristics."

"I did not."

"You put a frowning, lonely face on me." He reached up, tugged on her hair, and, like a magician — abracadabra — produced a pencil. Now she remembered, she'd stuck it behind her ear but obviously pushed it a bit too far in. Then he drew an ugly circle around the picture and put a slash through it.

Madeline took the paper from him and turned it around so he could see it.

"There's no frown."

His face flushed, his eyes flashed, and his jawline was so taut she wasn't sure he'd be able to open his mouth to talk. If she drew him now, she'd draw a wolf, a hungry wolf, a sad, hungry wolf. He looked at the picture. He looked back at her.

She said, as kindly as she knew how, "If you see sadness, that's you, not me. If you look at your sons and see insulting animal characteristics, you're projecting all of that. You need to figure out why a father would see that in his sons."

That wasn't the right thing to say, obviously. Tyler looked up from the sketch, his face a toxic mix of sadness and fury. "Don't tell me —"

"Ty, Doc, get up here." The constable's voice boomed down on them. "The coroner showed up. I need to talk to you both."

Tyler looked at the stairway; then he turned back, the sadness and confusion gone, leaving only rage. He leaned down until his nose almost touched hers.

"You stay away from my sons." He spent ten seconds apparently trying to burn her to a cinder with his eyes; then he turned and charged up the stairs.

Madeline trailed along, dismayed she'd alienated him. Just more evidence of her lack of people skills. Preoccupied with mentally giving herself a thrashing, she tripped on a step. She barked a shin, but her firm hold on the railing saved her from falling. Honestly, she hardly ever actually tumbled all the way to the bottom of a staircase.

She reached the top to see Constable Hammerstad whispering to Tyler, talking fast. The constable looked at her over Tyler's shoulder and abruptly ended the conversation.

Madeline approached them, wary of the officer's sharp eyes. As she got to Tyler's side, the constable caught her arm and turned her around. He took one wrist and she felt something cold, heard a metallic click.

"Dr. Madeline Stuart, you're under arrest for the murder of Melvin Melnik."

3

"You have the right to remain silent."

Maddy didn't even consider exercising that right.

"Whatever makes you think I killed that chap?" Handcuffed securely, she looked over her shoulder, expecting the constable to smile. This had to be a joke. She'd just gotten to town and the man looked as if he'd been dead for a while. Days maybe . . . quite stiff.

Maddy remembered that she'd been in town briefly several days ago. "I've never seen him before in my life. I only know his name because you said it."

Constable Junior didn't have one tiny cell of teasing on his face. Her stomach twisted as she realized the man was serious.

"We have reason for our suspicions." The constable finished shackling her and turned her to face him. They were still in her building, but through the door stood a crowd of onlookers. The caftan lady was in the forefront, smiling almost like she wanted to come up and thank Maddy for doing away with that man.

"You have the right to an attorney. If you cannot afford one —"

"I insist you unhand me this instant. I did not kill that man." And she couldn't afford a solicitor. As she faced the constable and the small gathering behind him, she saw Tallulah again immediately — hard to miss the explosion of color. Tallulah clutched the odd purse to her chest and . . . she seemed to be whispering to it. Most odd.

Beside Tallulah, a squared-faced woman in a white doctor's coat crouched in the doorway, obviously inspecting the body. What could this officer be thinking to accuse her?

The coroner lifted something up in a plastic bag. Maddy blinked when she recognized her favorite locket. She'd brought it with her other things a few days ago. Her parents' picture was inside; her name was clearly engraved on the back.

She remembered what the constable had said: *We have reason for our suspicions.* Now Madeline was looking at the reason.

"Let's go, Doc. We'll talk about this more at the station."

Madeline's heart stuttered as she walked into Tyler's building and slipped through the crowd, escorted by a firm grip on her elbow. She glanced back to see Tyler following and noticed Tallulah and Dora right behind him. Everyone fell into step. She was leading a parade. To jail. But once they got there, she'd be the only one on the business side of the bars.

A fair-haired woman snapped a picture. A tall man — so tidy Maddy's envy almost made her forget the handcuffs — stood at the blond's side. As Maddy led the parade downstairs, one curious person after another stared at her. Some said "hi" in such a friendly way that Maddy expected to be offered tea and crumpets.

At the base of the stairs, a gaunt vampire eyed her neck. She blinked her eyes and turned to the constable, whispering — although, as she recalled, vampires had excellent hearing — "Does Dracula live in Melnik, too?"

Her feet got twisted thanks to turning and walking at the same time. Predictable, really, upon reflection.

The constable, with the unlikely name of Cousin Junior, caught her arm. Tyler was behind Junior on the narrow stairs. He grabbed her around the waist to stop her from pinwheeling down the flight of steps. Once more upright, she again looked forward and realized she was face-to-face with the odd man, awake in the daytime, so that was a good sign. No, up close, definitely not a vampire, simply pale and dressed in black. A bit of a widow's peak. Not the walking dead at all.

Maddy hoped she wasn't developing a melancholy streak and seeing ghosts and monsters surrounding her.

The vampire said, "Hello." He reached out one hand — rude, that, Maddy thought, what with the handcuffs and all. When he realized she wasn't going to shake, he dropped his hand awkwardly. The bloodsucker turned to Junior.

"So who's dead? Can I have him? I'll bury him cheap." The man produced a card from the pocket of his black suit.

It wasn't "I vant to drink your blood," but it was very upsetting in its own way.

"Town mortician," Junior whispered in Maddy's ear. He must have sensed she was getting ready to run away screaming. "New here. Just digging up business. I admire a go-getter."

Junior took the card and moved her along. She didn't drag her feet a bit as they passed the vampire or as she greeted several men

44

wearing denim shirts and farmer caps. Jail was beginning to seem like a respite.

One of the men tugged on the bill of a green cap with a bright yellow deer on the front and said, "Hey, miss. Welcome to Melnik."

"Yes, a fine welcome." She frowned and the man smiled, mistaking her crankiness for wit, apparently.

Another man, with far too few teeth for his own good, and what appeared to be a bright red handkerchief tied over the top of his head like he was planning to protect his hair from paint — she'd heard them called do-rags — held her gaze. Not in an un-friendly way, but rather as if he had a partiality toward felonious women.

Thankfully they kept moving before he could ask for a wallet-sized copy of her mug shot.

As they passed him, he screamed. Maddy turned and saw the man gazing in horror at Tallulah's purse.

The do-rag man yelled, "Get that rat away from me!"

Maddy wanted to inquire as to the mean-ing of that, but Junior towed her onward.

They reached the door to the outside. She heard Tyler mutter to the constable, "New people in town. Dracula and the Hillbilly.

And a hillbilly that doesn't like Maxie. How's he gonna make a living?"

"Carrie hates Maxie, and she's doing okay."

"Yeah, but Carrie's got roots in Melnik."

Junior grunted. "There are other new folks, too. Melnik has really been growing."

Then Maddy saw the police car parked directly ahead.

She forgot about the odd townspeople as the reality of her waking nightmare returned. She'd heard of being arrested in a foreign country and locked away, no charges, forgotten in vermin-infested cells for years. Of course, those were usually third-world countries. But still . . .

"It occurs to me that you're not an American citizen, is that right, Doc? I'm not sure you have the right to an attorney."

Here it came. The gulag. The rats. The gruel. The torture. It scared her enough to make her testy. "Well, I definitely want one, and I can't afford one. So I'm not answering any questions until you figure that out."

"Fair enough. Tyler, I'm appointing you." Junior gave her a satisfied smirk. "Now I can question you."

Tyler stormed up alongside them. "I don't want to be her attorney, Cousin Junior. And it's a waste of time, anyway. You know she

46

didn't kill Melvin."

Junior opened the door of his black-and-white car. Maddy stumbled, but for once she wasn't being clumsy. This was from surprise.

"What is that?" She stared across the street.

"A grocery store." Junior stopped bustling her along.

"No, that statue. Is that Maxie dressed up like a — a —"

"He's wearing a T-shirt that says CUD-ELAK'S FINE FOOD GROCERY STORE." Tyler sounded proud.

"And pushing a shopping cart." Junior smiled fondly at the odd display.

"Do you think that's wise?" Maddy was rooting for Maxie to be important in this town, but really, mice did help spread the Black Plague — wouldn't that hurt sales?

"Of course it's wise. We're having an art festival. Look at what Olga did in front of the diner."

Junior courteously turned her, since her handcuffs made her movements awkward. Maddy saw a mouse, the same in size and shape as the grocery store statue, but this one wearing a chef's hat and apron. It stood proudly just down the sidewalk from Maddy, in front of a building that said JAN-

47

SOON'S Café, with the word SMORGASBORD painted beneath.

"Was that statue there when I was in town last Saturday?"

"Nope, we put him up on Sunday — it was the start of the art display." Junior nodded in satisfaction, pleased, by all appearances, by the massive rodent outside the diner. Only in Melnik was that an accomplishment of which to be proud. "We've got a whole bunch of 'em all over town."

"Well, that's charming, I'm sure." She was far from sure, but good manners seemed to require her to deviate from the truth in this instance.

Junior ushered her into his patrol car, using one hand to protect the back of her head. Madeline looked out the car windows. She knew the town had about a thousand residents. Half of them appeared to be filing out of Tyler's building to stare at her.

Once she was settled, Junior turned to Tyler. "We do not know she didn't kill Melvin. He had her locket clutched in his hand. That's conclusive evidence to me." Junior glared at Tyler. "You don't have the legal right to turn down a court appointment. Now get in the car."

"I do, too. I'm the acting county attorney. That means I'll be trying this case. I can't

48

be the prosecution and the defense on the same case."

Junior scowled then brightened. "We'll appoint a temporary county attorney. You're not even really official yet, anyway."

"I am, too. I got the appointment."

"You haven't had to try a case yet; that means it's not official. And I need a lawyer right here, right now. You're handy, so you're it. Get in."

Tyler crossed his arms.

Madeline noticed the car doors didn't have inside handles. "I don't want him as my solicitor. He doesn't even like me."

"Solicitor. Nice accent; I like it." Junior smiled at her, quite friendly, considering he'd just arrested her and accused her of murder. "Your agreement isn't required. You request an attorney, you get who I give you. Besides, he doesn't have to like you. No court-appointed attorney likes his clients."

"Forevermore, why not?" Madeline scooted toward the open door. If no one else was getting in, she'd just as soon stay outside, too.

Junior blocked her. Heading off an escape attempt, no doubt.

"Because they're all guilty." Tyler peeked into the car through the front passenger window.

"I'm not guilty!"

"I know."

Madeline leaned back in her seat, trying to figure out how she'd come to this. "How do you know?"

"You're not the type, that's how."

Was he saying she was too spineless to kill someone — even in a pinch? Offended, Madeline forced herself not to speak. What was she going to say — "I say, I'm tougher than I look. I could have done it"? No. Stupid. And her PhD — she was currently working on her second one — was a clear indication that she wasn't stupid. Except here she sat in handcuffs.

"So you're an anthropologist, huh?"

Maddy waited for Tyler to make some comment about digging up bones or pyramids. That's what she usually got. Perhaps an Indiana Jones question or two.

Before he could expose his ignorance, the constable jerked his thumb at the seat beside Maddy. "I've got another pair of cuffs, Ty. Defying my court order to represent her is actionable."

"Have you been watching *Law & Order* reruns again?"

Junior stepped aside. "Get in."

Tyler slid in, grumbling. He turned to her, the anger directed at the constable now, not her. But she remembered very well his order to stay away from his boys. Well, a jail cell ought to help her obey him.

He hated her.

Now he said she was innocent.

Madeline kept her head from spinning by sheer willpower.

"How do you know I'm innocent?"

"Well, anyone can look at you for two seconds and see you're a real nice lady. You'd never do a thing like that."

As a defense against a murder charge, it was quite weak. But it was so sweet. Her eyes filled with tears. "Thank you."

Constable Junior lowered himself behind the steering wheel. The car tilted to his side. The town clustered about so closely that Madeline wondered if Junior would have to threaten them before he could move the car.

"I didn't even know that man. Why would I have killed him? Don't I need . . ." Madeline searched through her mind for the word. She didn't watch much *Law & Order,* and most of a person's knowledge these days seemed to come from the telly.

"A motive," Tyler whispered. He raised his voice. "A motive, Junior. She was in town one day. The only possible motive she could have would be if Melvin just flat-out attacked her or something, and that would

51

be self-defense. She'd just run out onto the street screaming if that happened. C'mon. And means."

"Means?" Maddy whispered. "What is that?"

"Means is the weapon." He shook his head as though he found her hopeless as a murderess. To the constable he said, "You don't even know what killed him yet. There was no sign of a struggle. No gunshot wound. No outward sign of murder."

"Poison. In this town it's poison often as not."

Madeline turned to Tyler. "You have a preferred style of murder in Melnik?"

"No, of course not." Junior spoke too fast. "There's no crime in Melnik."

"This is the third murder in four years." Tyler shrugged. "But it's been the kind of murders that don't really count."

"What?"

"You know, personal. Not just general random murder like you'd have in a big city. And everyone who's dead had it coming to him, so they don't count."

Madeline cleared her throat. "So you're saying you only get killed in Melnik if you're bad?"

Junior and Tyler nodded.

"So just behave yourself and you'll be fine?"

"That seems to work for most people." Junior backed the car up with complete faith in the survival of the fittest. The crowd, obviously highly evolved, stepped aside.

"I've behaved myself all my life, and I'm not fine. I'm in handcuffs in the back of a police vehicle."

"Well, handcuffed isn't the same as murdered." Tyler looked at her, his eyes softening. "And I'll make sure you're fine."

The tears threatened again. "Thanks."

One spilled down her cheek, and Tyler wiped it away with a gentle thumb. "Don't cry. You're going to be all right. Trust me."

And she did. Why she trusted him, she couldn't say, but it was the absolute truth that she did. And that probably meant she was stupid despite her PhD, and she deserved to be under arrest.

No doubt if she'd been standing outside, she'd have remained in the same spot and let Junior drive right over her.

That's when she realized this might be the time for someone she trusted even more.

She closed her eyes and whispered a prayer. Nothing fancy. She had no time for eloquence. "Dear God, please be with me."

"You're a Christian?"

Madeline's eyes flickered open. "Yes."

"They have Christians in England?" Junior asked from the front seat.

Maddy narrowed her eyes at him. "Of course."

"I wasn't sure." Junior shrugged. "We hear weird things about Europe. Nude beaches, legalized drugs, rampant bad behavior."

"England is a lovely country, full of fine, upstanding people, many of them Christians, including me."

"That's good." Tyler sighed doubtfully. Or maybe he believed it about her, but not about the rest of England.

Madeline frowned. "It is good, since it's looking like I'll need a miracle to keep from going to prison."

"You don't need a miracle. You've got me, and you'll be fine. But praying wouldn't hurt. Do you have money for bail?"

They pulled up to the police station, and Junior hit the curb hard enough that she didn't get his question answered. It had been a drive of one and a half blocks. Americans! They drove everywhere.

Junior dragged his bulk out of the car and yanked open the door for them.

Madeline didn't have the money for bail. She'd impoverished herself with this extended trip to America.

Tyler got out and took her elbow. She tried to get to her feet with her hands restrained. Predictably, she fell on her face. Tyler's grip slipped, and she head-butted him in the stomach and knocked him backward into Cousin Junior. She sprawled flat on the ground, her fall broken by Tyler's body under hers.

Her glasses skittered off her face and she looked down at Tyler, nose to nose with the aggravating man. He shook his head and grinned. Her glasses were for distance, so having them off gave her a very clear view of his face. He really was adorable. A perfect specimen of the American male. She'd like to spend some time researching his smile. She looked closer because she hadn't seen much of it up to this point — not from such a short distance. But it was definitely more interesting than that ridiculous stuffed rodent.

She suddenly levitated. The constable had her by the waist. Tyler had her by the shoulders. The two of them set her on her feet. Junior fetched her spectacles and handed them to Tyler. He perched them on her nose while Junior shut the car doors and led the way inside.

Her vision was blurred, but she was certain that was from the constable's thumbprint on the lenses, rather than a concussion.

She remembered she was under arrest. She leaned closer to Tyler. "He won't hurt me, will he? I've heard of you Americans and your interrogation techniques. Beating people while others watch through two-way mirrors."

Tyler laughed. "Where'd you see that? A movie?"

"I'm not sure. Maybe. But everyone knows it's true."

"You'll be fine. Melnik can't afford a two-way mirror. Besides, it's my job to protect you, and Junior isn't inclined toward hitting anyone, least of all a pretty woman."

Pretty woman? She wasn't pretty; she was clumsy and studious and bad with people. A pariah, honestly. She wanted to ask him about it, maybe get him to say she was pretty again, just so she could store it in her memory to live on when times were tough. Like the time she'd set the university chancellor on fire, or spilled her coffee down the blouse of an elderly benefactor being wooed to donate to the college, or spent the entirety of a faculty party with a small piece of Swiss cheese stuck on her forehead.

Tyler had her upper arm in his grasp. It could be to block an escape attempt, but she rather thought it was to keep her on her feet.

"So do you have the money for bail?"

"That's an extremely rude question. You shouldn't inquire into my finances."

"Well, this is a murder investigation, and those have been known to stray into the area of rude. So don't tell me about your finances. Just tell me, if Junior gets the county judge to set your bail for a hundred thousand dollars, can you write a check for 10 percent of that?"

"No."

"Do you have a house to sign over as security so we can keep it if you skip town?"

"Of course not. But couldn't I just promise I won't run off?"

Tyler looked sideways at her. All his anger and grief were gone. The distraction of her being charged with murder had lightened his spirits. Well, she was glad to be of service. As they stepped up on the sidewalk, she noticed yet another large, decorated mouse. "Why is there an enormous mouse wearing a constable's uniform standing there?"

"It's a statue of Maxie."

"Forevermore, why?"

"Pay attention to the murder charges for a minute. I can tell you about the summer arts festival later. The reason we can't just take your word that you won't run off is, you'd be surprised how many murderers are liars, too. I've never heard any studies done on it, but I'm guessing it's, like, one hundred percent. So you might be a flight risk." Tyler held the door for her without letting go of her arm. The door opened into a small hallway with a door to the left that opened into a small, bare office with a boring gunmetal gray desk.

"No budget for a two-way mirror, indeed."

"You have no ties to the community."

"I've rented that building. That's the only home I've got right now. I've got a nonrefundable ticket to return to London in early September and no money to buy a different ticket or even pay the fee to have the departure date changed."

"Still, unless we can convince Junior to drop these charges, you'll have to pay bail or stay in custody."

Tyler settled her into a chair and only released her arm at that point. He pulled up a matching folding chair with a dull scrape of the legs on the cement floor and sat beside her.

The constable unlocked her shackles and sat behind his desk. "Now how well did you know Melvin Melnik?"

Maddy groaned.

4

Tyler could feel his will weakening.

He'd have to put up bail. He had a house. He had plenty of money.

But that wasn't the way a savvy lawyer worked. Still, Dr. Snow White was innocent, and his conscience wouldn't allow him to leave her locked up.

If he didn't pay, she might spend the night, possibly the whole summer, locked up awaiting trial. On the other hand, rustic as it was, the jail cell looked more comfortable than that building she'd rented. He'd noticed an inflatable mattress, twin-sized. That was about the extent of her creature comforts.

Then Dr. Notchke came into the police station with her preliminary report and started right in talking. "When is this town going to get good cell phone service?" The doctor didn't wait for an answer. "Based on the condition of the body, I'd say he's been dead twelve to twenty-four hours. And I suspect his hand was pried open after death and the locket stuck in deliberately. Someone framed Dr. Stuart."

Tyler saw tears well in Dr. Snow's eyes. He resisted the urge to give her a hug.

"I can absolutely prove I wasn't in Melnik twelve to twenty-four hours ago." She sniffled, and he handed her a handkerchief. "I was doing final exam work at the university. My study group and I have worked day and night for the last week finishing a project that was overdue. I wasn't alone for a second."

"I've gotta go." Dr. Notchke set her handwritten notes on Junior's desk. "It's pinochle night at the VFW Hall in Fremont. Try not to find any more dead bodies for a while, eh, Junior?" Dr. Notchke didn't wait around for a protest.

Junior studied the papers, looking disgruntled. "Well, I'm not buying your alibi just because you've said you have one."

"Oh, rubbish. You should be thrilled I can prove I'm innocent." Dr. Snow rose to her feet, sounding testy.

Tyler braced himself to save her. Any little distraction on her part and she usually ended up knocking someone over. The woman just needed to concentrate full-time

61

on staying upright.

"Why's that?" Junior looked up from his scribbling.

Maddy laid both hands flat on Junior's desk with a muffled growl. "Because I'm innocent, you daft man! You don't want to arrest someone who's innocent, do you?"

"Well, closing a case is always nice." Junior tapped his notebook with his stubby pencil.

Tyler did his best not to laugh. Junior really preferred to run a tidy police force. He and two part-time deputies. If there was a dog off its leash, Junior was there. If a carload of teenagers did wheelies on the football field, Junior put a stop to it. If someone threw a punch over a bowling score, Junior had a jail cell, and he wasn't afraid to use it.

But murder? Tyler knew his second cousin Junior Hammerstad — or possibly his first cousin once removed; there was some dispute over that — had never signed on for this. The fact that he'd closed two earlier murder cases in quick time had given him a false sense of his own detecting skills, which, to Tyler's way of thinking, were non-existent.

Tyler had been a lawyer in Omaha for five years before Liza died, and mostly he'd reviewed contracts for his firm's huge corporate clients. That was the kind of lawyer Liza had wanted him to be. But in the year before he landed that job, he'd done a lot of cases as a court-appointed attorney for the city of Omaha. Tyler knew about real crime and real detective work. The crime here, murder, was real enough, but the detective work . . . not so real.

In an abandoned room like the one Melvin was in, Junior should have had good luck finding trace evidence. But he'd allowed — or rather been unable to stop — the whole town from marching up to take turns looking at the body. There should have been footprints in the dust. Of course, his boys had been up there, but those prints would be easy to identify. Tyler's and Dr. Snow's had only been in that one corner. But Junior hadn't kept the good citizens of Melnik out, and now anyone could claim that any matching hairs or prints came after the crime was discovered.

Tyler hoped whoever had stuffed Melvin in the cupboard came forward and confessed. Otherwise, this could be a hard crime to solve and a failure that would make poor old Junior feel bad.

Tyler felt bad, too. "So why my building? Was someone trying to frame me and Dr. Snow?"

"Who?" His client's dark, perfectly arched brows lifted above her glasses.

Tyler moved on fast. "If Dr. Stuart's locket was put there postmortem, maybe it started out to be a frame-up on me. Then they found her stuff and had a better idea."

"Or maybe" — Junior consulted his notebook — "Melvin was living there and that dictated the site of the crime. He hid out in Gunderson's house a long time. Maybe he came back to town, saw Joe and Bonnie had that house opened up wide, leaving him nowhere to ghost around, so he immediately picked another deserted building and just snuck in. He's only been out of jail a week."

"Then whoever killed him must have known he was there or found him there. We need a motive."

"Lots of motive for killing Melvin. Everyone in town hates him for filing that suit to gain custody of Maxie."

The clumsy doctor leaned forward. "Custody of Maxie?"

Why would this woman care about Maxie? Tyler sure knew he didn't, despite Bonnie's loyalty to that dumb, obese vermin.

"Someone is trying to take possession of that rodent you all worship?"

"We don't worship him, for Pete's sake." Tyler stood beside her. Better to catch her when she fell. "He's a town mascot. We use him to try to draw attention to Melnik. It gives us an excuse to have a summer celebration and a Christmas parade. Every little town has something like that."

She smiled. "Poor choice of words. So sorry."

Tyler needed a pocket calculator with a memory function to keep track of all of Dr. Snow's "So sorry's." "Let's get back to the case. I'm sure the doc was just a convenient patsy."

"I say, that sounds ominous." She adjusted her glasses. "Very Cosa Nostra, actually."

"Yeah, right. The mob." Tyler laughed. "Anyway, we've accused so many people of murder in this town, they're starting to resent it. Joe, Tallulah, Shayla, Hal. You even suspected Bonnie for a while, remember, Junior?"

"All of them but Joe and Bonnie confessed." Junior scowled. "It's not like they've got a reason to resent being suspected. And they all did kill Wilkie; they just didn't kill him dead."

"What?" Dr. Snow adjusted her glasses and nearly knocked them off her face.

Tyler and Junior both ignored her. It just took too long to bring her up to speed.

"Besides, I never believed for a second

65

Bonnie killed Gunderson, and you know it."

Tyler nodded. "Still, I think we should proceed with caution. The obvious suspects are, again, Tallulah and Bonnie. I mean, no one was more upset about the thought of losing Maxie than they were."

"Bonnie? Your very pregnant sister?" The good doctor regained her seat and crossed her legs, resting her right ankle on her left knee. Her baggy clothing almost swallowed her as she leaned forward, her wrists resting on her ankle, her expression ridiculing him and Junior both. "You think she tucked Mr. Melnik up inside that cupboard and left him there for you or your young lads to find? Quite rude, actually. Plus heavy lifting for a woman in such an advanced state of pregnancy."

Junior scratched his pencil in his notebook. Tyler had a sneaking suspicion he was crossing off Bonnie's name. Grudgingly, Tyler gave Junior credit. The man didn't list suspects based on personal feelings.

"Physically, she isn't capable of packing him away, even if she killed him up there. But she had a motive, Ty. Plus opportunity. I'll bet there's a key in city hall, and Bonnie's in and out of that building all the time."

"Give it up. She's innocent and so is Tallulah. Tallulah's a drama queen. That means she can act, or thinks she can. You heard her screaming with joy over Melvin being dead. No way does a murderer choose that for her false reaction."

"So who?" Junior chewed on his eraser. "Everyone and no one."

"Who stands to gain from this poor chap's death?"

Tyler almost grinned. He really was enjoying her company. And she was cranky. He'd noticed that and still enjoyed her. Although she wasn't cranky when she was in handcuffs. She'd been vulnerable and sweet and teary-eyed then. Liza had known how to fake being sweet and sad and vulnerable, too. She'd proved it before they were married. She hadn't wasted much time wheedling afterward. She just issued orders.

Tyler smirked. "You have been watching American movies."

"England has a movie industry, too, you know." She scowled.

"Anthony Hopkins acting stiff. Old ladies named Dame Whatever impersonating some queen. Shakespeare. No interrogation techniques there. What else you got?"

"The case, sir? Have you forgotten?"

Strangely enough, he had forgotten. Tyler

67

turned back to Junior. "Melvin got a piece of the town's settlement after we took Gunderson's ill-gotten gains. He didn't get it at first, because we didn't know he was alive. When he turned up, Shayla had already spent hers, so we cut a portion from Rosie — she's in jail; what does she need money for? — and took a chunk out of the trust funds for Donette's baby and Kevin. Plus we made Hal give some of his share back. All of them were mad about coughing up the cash."

"Melvin thought the city should have made up the last slice Shayla owed him, but we weren't about to." Junior nodded. "And Joe had Gunderson's money, but he wasn't liable, and since Melvin killed Gunderson, letting Melvin profit from his death was illegal. He'd been using the money he did get to pay his lawyer to delay the murder case. He was also suing Shayla for her share, and he filed papers to get custody of Maxie."

"Melvin wanted the mouse?" The fairy princess doctor rested her chin on her hand and folded up over herself, studying him and Junior like they were lab rats.

Tyler ignored her. "Now that Melvin's dead, unless we find a will, his money — whatever's left of it — should be divided between Kevin, Hal, and Donette's baby."

68

"Shayla might want a cut. She didn't kick into the pot, but she's family, so it might count legally as an inheritance rather than just paying back his cut of the settlement." Junior shook his head. "Kevin didn't do it. He just graduated from high school this spring. He got a scholarship to Wayne State. Since he's been living with the Andersons, he's turned into a fine young man."

"The apple doesn't fall far from the tree." Tyler leaned back, pondering. His metal chair creaked.

"And those Melniks are one twisted fruit salad, no doubt about that." Junior nodded and made a note. "I'll talk to Kevin, but I hate to upset him. Doubt Donette's little one did it; he's only four."

"Since Hal and Donette are married, they'd stand to gain the most, though, since they had two shares. Hal's and the baby's."

With a grudging look on his face, Junior made a note. "Hal's all right. No way he did this, but I'll leave his name on the list."

"That leaves Shayla. She's got the spine to kill someone; we know that."

"How do you know that?" The doctor was paying rapt attention, leaning forward over her bent knee, hanging on every word.

Tyler found her interest unusual. Except for those few minutes when she was accused of the crime, why did any of this matter to her? Didn't she have a paper to write? "We know that because she poisoned her father, Wilkie Melnik, when she was eighteen. Someone else killed Wilkie before the poison could finish him off, but Shayla had the cold in her blood to pour that antifreeze into her father's beer."

Junior nodded. "As far as I know, she's not in town. I heard she's living over in Gillespie. The coroner's doing a toxicology report, and she suspects poison. Why not antifreeze?"

"Gillespie is close enough for Shayla to have driven over here. She could have even been in contact with Melvin. They could have conspired to gain custody of Maxie with plans to extort the town. Lots of people would pay generously to keep that mouse."

"Joe knows how much it means to Bonnie."

"Bonnie, your sister, right?"

Tyler felt a little sorry for the good doctor. She was trying to keep up. "Yes, pregnant Bonnie, the one you met a little while ago. Her husband, Joe, inherited Maxie then donated him to the town before Melvin sued for custody."

"Well, it's a little more complicated than that," Junior interrupted.

"Of course it is." Maddy sounded resigned and exhausted. Who could blame her?

"Joe actually had to throw Maxie away."

"What?"

"I fished him out of the trash." Junior said it with such pride that Tyler didn't point out that he sounded like a lunatic. "It gave the whole case some shaky points, and Melvin was exploiting that."

Tyler went back to the crime. "Melvin might have been planning on holding Maxie for ransom. Joe might have paid, too. He'd do anything for my sister."

"Isn't *custody* a term used between divorcing parents?" Maddy asked. "Surely there is no custody of a dead mouse. And ransom — that's about kidnapping . . . a human being."

Tyler almost snickered. They'd left the doc behind, and that was a fact.

She must have detected his amusement, because she got huffy, and that reminded him of Liza. She unbent her long legs, so slender she should have been as fleet and graceful as a gazelle. As she stood, she stepped on the cuff of her baggy slacks, cut in manly tailored lines but insanely loose, and fell forward against Junior's desk, knocking his notebook straight into his ample gut.

"So sorry." She reached for the notebook, caught a pencil holder by accident, and sent pencils and pens clattering to the floor beside Junior.

Junior reached for the sky in surrender. "I'll get the pens."

She stood upright without assistance. "So, you've decided it must be this Shayla person, then?"

Tyler looked at Junior. Neither of them answered.

"You've just said she's the only serious suspect."

Junior nodded. "Well, she's serious all right. But it's a little early to be setting our minds on one person. There are other new folks in town."

"Besides me?" The doc stood straighter as if she didn't feel so alone.

"What about the vampire mortician? Hard to forget him." Tyler shrugged one shoulder.

"Hard is right. Believe me, I've tried. Weird dude. Name's Dolph Torkel. But a guy's not a murderer just because he looks goofy. I've heard he's fresh out of undertaker college. We needed him in Melnik, but we only know what little he's told us about his background. I could sniff around there."

"Dolph?" Maddy asked. "As in Adolph?"

Junior shrugged. "I suppose. Funny how

the name Adolph fell out of favor after Hitler, huh? Just wrecked the name."

"Funny," Maddy said dryly.

"And how about that antique shop?" Tyler wanted to stay on track. "That lady isn't normal. I've only met her a couple of times, just in passing, but she seems to have a vacancy in her brain. Always singing and dancing — she looks high as a kite to me. Like the flower child that time forgot. Name's Moonbeam something. Ask Dora. If she's drug-involved, she could have some connection to Melvin through prison. They might have mutual acquaintances."

Junior made a note. "The new plumber has only been here a couple of months, and Dora can't get a thing out of him."

"The guy with all the missing teeth?" Tyler asked.

"Yep."

Tyler couldn't control a shudder. "I was ready for him to start twanging the *Deliverance* theme on a banjo."

"Jamie Bobby Wicksner, and don't be calling him Jamie or Jim or Jimmy. He likes the whole Jamie Bobby. Nice enough guy, I suppose, if you can keep from staring at his teeth." Junior grimaced. "He graduated from tech school and he's already done a few plumbing jobs around town. Nick double-checked his work and said he knows what he's doing."

"Well." Maddy dusted her hands. "Good to see you've got lots of people to investigate. Am I free to go? I need to settle in."

"You're still going to live up there?" Tyler could still see Melvin's body, stiff, eyes open, dead as dead could be. He wasn't even sure he'd be able to practice law in that building, let alone sleep there as Dr. Snow planned to do.

A little worry line appeared between her eyebrows, but she shrugged. Her blouse flowed over her body, and her pants dropped from her armpits to her hips. She tugged them back up. "Where else? I can't afford to rent another flat."

"But you'll be sleeping right next door to a crime scene. Whoever murdered Melvin might come back. Your door isn't that sturdy. If you'd have moved in there yesterday, you might have been killed, too, just to silence you as a witness."

Dr. Snow's eyes widened, her shoulders slumped, and her pants dropped. "I hadn't thought of that." She shook her head. Her ponytail holder must have broken, because her hair cascaded around her shoulders. She scraped it back, hooking the dark silk behind her ears and leaving a new trail of dirt with her fingertips. She found several of the pencils, stared at them, and stuck two behind each ear. Then she turned to the door. "Well, let's hope whoever killed him was a one-off, because it's the only home I've got."

She opened Junior's door without incident and left.

"Piesforsale."

Tyler leapt to his feet. "She'll either fall into Clara's pies or not know she's supposed to buy one. Either way, Clara will get mad."

He ran outside.

"NoonestarveswhileI'maround." Crazy Clara, the Mad Baker of Melnik, stood with her cart full of horrible pies.

Tyler knew his duty. He bought a pork chop and coconut shaving cream pie. Junior got a radish and paper clip meringue. The anthropologist gagged and hurried up the street with her hand over her mouth, nearly falling over the Maxie statue in the process. Tyler straightened Maxie's police cap and chased after her.

She stepped off the curb and nearly fell down a gutter into Melnik's sewer system. It wasn't big enough for her to slip through, but somehow Tyler thought if anyone could manage it, it'd be Maddy. She saved herself before he got there, and Tyler had to admit the woman had grown to adulthood some-how.

He extended a key ring to her. "This is for my building. Your cell isn't going to work."

"Cell? Are we talking about biology?"

"Cellular phone. You're really cut off from everyone. Nothing is open on Main Street in the evening. You don't have a home phone and cell phones don't work. You'd have trouble getting help."

"I don't need help."

"Anyone might need help. This is the key to the front door of my building. I think it works in the upstairs door, too. But we might have left that unlocked, anyway." Tyler couldn't remember. Locking doors wasn't a high priority in Melnik. After all, there was no crime in Melnik. "There's a phone downstairs. My home number is taped to the desk. If you need anything, call me."

She looked from the key ring to Tyler and back. When her eyes lifted the next time, he thought he saw a gleam of tears. Why would access to a phone make a woman cry?

"And don't forget in an emergency to call 911."

"Oh yes. What was the number again?"

Tyler shook his head and told her. "Seriously, try to memorize it."

"I will. Perhaps if I write it down. Thank you very much. I doubt I'll need it, but it's very kind of you."

Tyler almost regretted his generosity, because looking in those shiny, bright blue eyes, framed with lashes so long they fluttered in the breeze, made him forget all the hard lessons he'd learned about women. "Well, I'm your lawyer, so I'm the logical one to call if you need anything."

She looked at the key in her hand. "Oh, right, my lawyer. Of course." The silence lasted too long. She dashed at her eyes and smeared dirt, now damp enough to qualify as mud, on her cheeks and nose. "Well, thank you." She turned and hurried off.

Tyler couldn't tear his eyes away. She reached the intersection with Main Street. Tyler held his breath, hoping she didn't cross the street at the same time Dora drove by. Not exactly the irresistible force meeting the immovable object. More like the clumsy princess and the blind bat.

In short, a fractured fairy tale — with real fractures.

Dr. Snow rounded the building, and just before she disappeared, she stopped and glanced back. For a second, or maybe three seconds or ten. She looked him right in the eye.

Tyler's heart hurt from that pretty, klutzy doctor looking at him.

She turned, smacked her shoulder into the bricks of the old furniture store, and vanished around the corner in a cloud of sparkling fairy dust. Or maybe that was mortar from the building she'd almost knocked down and the sparkles were in Tyler's eyes.

He'd had seven years of college, he'd passed the bar and worked in a high-pressure corporate office for five years, and still . . . he didn't have a brain in his head.

That wasn't a discovery he was making right now. He'd known for a long, long time. He'd suspected before the end of his honeymoon. He'd only known Liza two months when they eloped. He'd phoned Bonnie and told her after the fact.

The fact that hurting Bonnie hadn't shamed him was a cross he'd always bear. The fact that Liza had started with her slights aimed at his family and his embarrassing hometown had been major clues to his idiocy.

But then, a month into their marriage, Liza had announced she was pregnant.

That feeling of being trapped after four

weeks of marriage hit him like a two-by-four. If he'd been a coyote, he'd have gnawed his foot off to get away. But he was a man; he'd made vows before God. And here was a defenseless baby. That's when he knew how badly he regretted his choice for a wife. He'd married quicksand, and Liza had sucked him under hard and fast.

The hurt in his chest right now, from the doctor's glance, reminded him how fast he'd fallen in love last time, how stupid he was about women, and how completely he couldn't trust his feelings. He was grateful for the reminder. He turned back to Junior and, since Clara had gone on her way, extended his pie to his cousin. "Toss this for me, okay? I'm going to find the boys."

Junior balanced his own pie on one hand. "Do it yourself. You bought it; you throw it out. You know the rules."

Those really were the rules. Unwritten, but known by everyone. You had to buy a pie because Clara needed the money. And you had to throw it away yourself. Tyler hadn't been out of Melnik that long.

Junior leaned forward to sniff Tyler's pie. "You've got to give Clara points for creativity. I think she used menthol shaving cream on this one. Kind of refreshing."

Tyler rolled his eyes.

Junior smirked as he bounced the radish and paper clip pie on his fingertips. Not one bit worried he might drop it. "The doc sure is a pretty little thing. Clumsy, though. A man could keep busy his whole life saving her from one disaster or another."

Tyler wondered how long he'd stared after Maddy. Maybe Junior, the old coot, had some detecting skills after all. "Are you done assigning me to cases I don't want?"

Junior shrugged. "For now. But don't leave town." He laughed at his cop humor all the way back to his office, leaving Tyler with an aching heart, bitter memories, and a pork chop and coconut shaving cream pie.

There wasn't enough menthol in the world to make him feel better.

What had he been thinking to come home? Just more proof he was an idiot.

5

Moving to Melnik was a stroke of genius.

The town was fascinating and growing on Maddy with each passing second.

Even the arrest had been quite educational. Now, without the handcuffs, she was able to see the benefits of the experience. The constable had taken her word on an alibi. He might well check it out, but mostly he seemed to have decided to let her go because Tyler said, "She wouldn't do a thing like that."

How trusting. What a lovely little town.

She finished her settling in, double-checked the lock on her adjoining doors to Tyler's building — she found a second door downstairs as well and locked that — and headed to Jansson's for supper. A community gathering place. She'd begin getting to the heart of this town full of lovable mouse-worshipping lunatics.

As she emerged from her building, she

studied Melnik's business district. One block long. To her left was Tyler's law office. She lived straight across the street from the grocery. She strolled along, reading storefronts. Melnik Historical Society Museum, Melnik City Hall and Fire Department — where the ambulance had originated, most likely. Next, a lovely shaded rock garden scattered with benches. Odd to have a gap like that in a row of buildings.

Next she passed O'Connor Construction, the words neatly painted on the window. O'Connor was the name of the other woman Maddy wanted to meet. Carrie O'Connor. Could this be her family? Was it possible that everyone worked within a few feet of her? Well, why not? Honestly, the whole town was within a few feet of her.

Maddy noticed a building across the street with THE BUGLE painted on the front window. The town newspaper where Carrie O'Connor worked. The building looked dark, so Maddy didn't cross over.

The next business past O'Connor Construction was an antique store. A plain rectangle of cheap printer paper, hand-lettered with MOONBEAM'S ANTIQUITIES, was taped to the glass front door. That was the only identification of the business. Through the window, a woman dressed like an aging hippie danced as she flicked a feather duster over glassware. Maddy saw her raise one arm and open and close her hand. There were tiny cymbals on her fingers.

Next was a rather ghastly front window display. A casket. On sale. A large hand-printed sign taped to the coffin said:

$499 PLUS TAX
EMBALMING, HAIR, AND MAKEUP
NOT INCLUDED

Startled, she stopped to stare. Read the fine print.

Maddy had never heard of a coffin sale before. After she'd stood far too long, she raised her eyes, jumped, and heard herself squeak, quite embarrassing. The local vampire stood behind the coffin. With a quick smile — which he returned with a little wave — she moved on. As she passed his door, she read TORKEL'S FUNERAL HOME painted high on the window. Oh yeah, little Adolph. Not a vampire. Not a sign of fangs anywhere when he'd smiled.

She remembered Dolph was a suspect, although based on absolutely nothing except his oddness and newness in town. Not fair, that. He moved so he could see her through the door and waved at her more vigorously. She was struck by the notion that he might be lonely. She could certainly relate.

She waved back, suspecting God would have her invite the chap to dinner. Well, she didn't rule it out for the future, but not tonight. She moved quickly on, embarrassed to be caught staring. Yet if a bargain-basement coffin stood in your window, you had not a single leg to stand on if you complained about people staring.

The next building was the restaurant. Food and coffins — not a comfortable marriage.

Jansson's Café and Smorgasbord. How utterly charming. A Swedish eatery, decorated with Dala horses. Maddy had traveled to Sweden and recognized the little wooden carving of a horse, painted bright red and decorated with a harness and saddle in ribbons of blue, green, and yellow. A lovely bit of Europe in middle America. It was delightful, except for the four-foot statue of a mouse wearing a chef's hat standing on the sidewalk.

Bad show all around, that. An appalling lapse of judgment, really. This close she noticed a spatula tucked in Maxie's little paw. Setting her disgust aside, she knew it would add color to her thesis, so she determined to come back and take pictures. No one would believe her if she just wrote the details in her paper.

On the door, right above a wooden sign that said VÄLKOMMEN, was stenciled a cartoon of a stout man wearing red overalls and a red cowboy hat. The words HERBIE HUSKER rather ruined the Swedish effect, but Maddy had been in Nebraska long enough to know that the University of Nebraska football team's mascot, Herbie Husker, was far and away more of an iconic figure than Maxie Mouse. Perhaps she'd study him for her next doctorate.

She had a few quid in her pocket, American dollars, of course. She wasn't stonebroke. Even though her present flat was reasonably priced — with first and last month's rent and a damage deposit — she didn't have funds to rent another flat. But she could eat a meal out now and again if she so chose.

A bell tinkled overhead as she entered the establishment. The tinkle for some reason reminded her that Tyler had called her Dr. Snow. What in heaven's name had that been about?

She forgot all about it when a mouthwatering aroma greeted her like a mother's hug. Pastry and roasting meat, sautéed

85

onions and brewing coffee. Heavenly.

Maddy realized she'd yet to eat today. The quiet murmur of voices and steady clink of silverware stopped. A fair-sized crowd, scattered about at the square tables and booths, turned and stared. Beastly rude in most places, but apparently not so in Melnik. Maddy had been stared at virtually nonstop since she'd arrived. She reached for her notebook to document the "staring allowed" culture and found the book missing.

Right when she needed to take notes most! Well, she was a twit and that came as no surprise, even with papers saying she had a PhD and the bills saying she was paying to earn a second one.

She wondered how hard it would be to find folks in this charming hamlet who would allow her to interview them. Awfully hard, she suspected. She'd heard small towns tended to be cliquish. Made worse by her implication in murder. Add in her dismal record with interpersonal relationships and the fact that, while she might have God's grace in her soul, she lacked grace utterly in all other ways. When God had been splicing in the coordination gene, Maddy had obviously gotten in the wrong line and picked up two left feet. This summer promised to be one long struggle. One long, lonely struggle. Much like her whole life.

A handprinted sign told her to seat herself, so she slid into an empty booth, depressed to be eating alone. Wishing she had her notebook so she could sit and doodle and ignore her loneliness.

A woman charged the table. It took Maddy a second, but she recognized her from the murder scene.

"Hi, I'm Dora."

The plump matron sat down across from Maddy, turned, and bellowed, "Coffee, Olga!"

A woman, taller and broader than Dora but just as gray, was already approaching the table with a thermal pot. "I'm way ahead of you, Dora."

The aproned woman smiled a motherly smile at Maddy. She limped as if her joints hurt. "First cup of my coffee's on the house. Then you'll be hooked, and you're mine for life."

Olga and Dora chuckled — an inside joke, it appeared.

"Do you want the smorgasbord, or do you want to order off the menu?" Olga finished filling the cup, and the fragrant coffee made Maddy — a tea drinker in the normal course of things — suspect "being Olga's

87

for life" wasn't a joke.

"I . . . I . . ." Maddy had never been in a restaurant before when she hadn't had plenty of time to think, unless it had golden arches.

"Give her the smorgasbord; she'll need her strength." Dora reached across the table and patted Maddy's hand. "Now tell me about yourself. Did you kill Melvin? He had it coming. I heard Junior let you go. Got away with it, huh? Bad business killing people. No sense making a habit of it. But Junior didn't like Melvin. Must have decided to look the other way this once. Providing you stop, I expect this'll be the end of it."

Maddy shook her head. "I didn't kill him. I've been set free. I had an alibi."

Dora beamed. "Good thinking. Honestly, with all the murders in this town, it'd be wise to keep someone with you at all times. To protect yourself if you're the next victim and to have a handy alibi if you look suspicious. Unless the person you kept with you was also the murderer." Dora fell silent, rubbing her chin, trying to solve the alibi dilemma. A quick glance at Maddy sharpened Dora's already-keen focus. "Pencils in your hair, girl."

Maddy felt her cheeks heat. She'd always

blushed like a schoolgirl. She began plucking the pencils out, astounded at how many
she found.

Leaning close, Dora added, "You really
could use one of those whitening tooth-
pastes. What was your name again? You're a
doctor? This town could use a doctor. Madeline, right? I've got bursitis in one shoulder
that's the bane of my existence."

Maddy closed her mouth then tried to talk
and conceal her yellow teeth at the same
time. "I'm Dr. Madeline Stuart. I'm not a
medical doctor."

Maddy had seven pencils on the table in
front of her. She quit talking as she contem-
plated the disaster of her being put in
charge of fragile, sick people. It didn't bear
thinking about. "I've spent the last half year
in Omaha studying for a second doctorate
in anthropology. My first doctorate was in
cultural —"

"Dinosaur bones?" Dora nodded. "It's a
wonder they haven't found all of those yet.
I mean, how many can there be? Good
grief, it's like you can't turn around without
tripping over a tyrannosaurus."

Maddy opened her mouth to straighten
that out, aware that her yellow teeth must
be glaring like a caution light.

Another woman slid in beside Dora. The

caftan lady. Tallulah. Maddy couldn't believe her luck. Except for her horrid teeth and the pencils, this was going well.

"I heard Junior let you off on the murder rap." Tallulah seemed to suggest Maddy had gotten away with it, rather than being found completely innocent.

"I didn't kill him."

Tallulah shrugged, adjusted her turban, and lifted one open hand.

Maddy jumped.

A mouse. A very large mouse — his nasty teeth bared — sat in Tallulah's hand.

"You've saved Maxie." Tallulah spoke with the melodrama of a Broadway actress, projecting her voice to the cheap seats. "And you've saved the town of Melnik." Tallulah's arms swept wide and buried Dora's head in flowing fabric.

Dora batted at the curtain of rayon hanging in her face. "Can't you at least put elastic on the wrists? You've got mashed potatoes and gravy on your arm again. And just because they've invented deodorant, Tallulah, there's no reason not to take a bath now and then."

Maddy noticed Tallulah didn't even react to the insults. Perhaps it wasn't only Maddy who caught the sharp edge of Dora's tongue.

Focus on the rodent. The famed Maxie, at last.

Maddy realized she wasn't particularly fond of mice. She hadn't been around that many, not outside a lab, and she'd never given them much thought. She could abide them, but not as dinner guests. And yet here was the renowned mouse of Melnik. What an opportunity!

She'd just eat later, perhaps at a different table. Which table had Tallulah come from? She wished she could be sure so she could avoid that table, too.

"So tell me about Maxie. It seems . . ." She chose her words carefully, remembering how Tyler had snapped at her when she'd said "worship". She believed they did worship this mouse, or at least held him in awe to an extent that bordered on religious zeal. Not Tyler, perhaps, but many of Melnik's residents.

"It seems that you . . . revere him."

A bell sounded, and Maddy heard the door open behind her. She planned to stare, since it seemed like the town tradition. But Tallulah drew her attention with a wide flourish of Maxie.

"He is the symbol of our greatness." Tallulah lifted Maxie over her head, and her voice rose in triumph and wonder and, yes . . . worship. "He has brought the town back from the brink of the grave. Maxie single-handedly snatched us from the jaws of death."

"Oh, surely not." Maddy glanced at Dora. With a start she realized the older woman seemed intent on boring a hole into Maddy's brain with her eyes.

Tallulah continued emoting. "He has rejuvenated our businesses, given the town youth, and is helping build a future for one and all."

He has given the town youth? Like some fertility symbol? Well, mice were known to be fruitful and multiply to an appalling extent, so as a symbol it made an icky kind of sense. Maddy longed for her notebook.

"His life, his eminence, his regal size are —"

"Get that mouse out of here, Tallulah, or I promise you, I'm calling the county health department." The slim blond woman who'd taken Maddy's picture at the murder scene stood far back from the table, turned, and yelled at the kitchen. "You hear me, Olga? You tell her to put Maxie back in his cage at the museum. I've got the number on speed dial and you know it. I'll march right down to Bonnie and Joe's and crouch behind his car and phone. You know I'm serious; I've done it before."

The patrons chuckled and settled in to watch the show.

Mice, yelling, threats — quite odd.

Tallulah rose before Olga said a word. The young blond backed up until she pressed up against a tall, dark-haired man who had a towheaded toddler on one hip. The man, neat as a pin and handsome as a knight in shining armor, slipped his spare arm around the blond's waist. Maddy had noticed him before at the arrest, and the blond had taken a snapshot.

The man spoke quietly. "Carrie, you're going to have to hold Heather if you jump."

"Please, Tallulah, go up the far side of the diner. Nick has his hands full." The blond had her eyes riveted on the mouse as she spoke.

Despite a gleam of temptation in Tallulah's eyes, she kept well away from the newcomers. Once Tallulah headed for the exit in a huffy swirl of fabric and mouse fur, the blond turned her attention to Maddy.

"Do you mind staying and eating with us . . . at another table?" Carrie twisted her hands together and glanced nervously at the spot where Tallulah and Maxie had been, then looked right back at the retreating Tallulah as if her eyes were drawn to the mouse by powerful magnets.

Dora snorted. "Maxie is perfectly clean, Carrie. Stop being silly. You need to spend time with Maxie if you're ever going to get over this foolish little fear. I thought you'd been working on it. Are you any better?"

"I hate mice with the fire of a thousand suns." Carrie still watched the mouse.

Maddy doubted that Carrie thought the mouse would jump at her, but she had no such confidence in Tallulah.

With a sniff of disdain, Tallulah swung open the door, working her exit like she was onstage at London's West End, bucking for an Olivier Award. "You remind me of your great-grandma Bea more every day." She slammed the door on her way out. The tinkling bell rang joyfully.

Carrie settled at a table across the way and gave Maddy a hopeful look. Of course, Maddy didn't hesitate. She turned to Dora. "If you'll pardon me?"

Without waiting for an answer — afraid of what Dora might find fault with now — Maddy picked up her pencils, gratefully abandoned the mouse hairs, and walked to the new table. This had to be the Carrie O'Connor she was looking for. What luck! All three of her primary targets in one day. Although Carrie's reaction to the rodent didn't bode well for her being one of the believers. And honestly, Maddy was quite sure she'd met nearly everyone in town in one day. So why not her primary targets?

Nick sat beside Carrie, still holding the baby. The child picked up the silverware and tried to put the fork in her mouth. Nick grabbed it before the tike could put her eye out.

Dora slid in beside Maddy, using her ample bum to shove Maddy sideways. "You need to try harder to keep that baby clean, Carrie. It'll be a wonder if she lives to adulthood. Germs, germs everywhere. Nothing will kill them better than a good pine cleaner."

"This from a woman having coffee with a mouse." Carrie rolled her eyes.

"We're using pine cleaner, Dora." The man chucked the little girl under the chin, and the toddler twisted to give him a heart-stopping grin. "And lots of bleach and that antiseptic hand wash and —"

The little girl patted the man's chin, imitating him. He hugged her and kissed her neck. She giggled. Carrie watched, her smile as wide as the child's. Maddy noticed her own smile, and Dora's.

Maddy felt better about her teeth when Dora insulted the very tidy parents of this very tidy baby. Which reminded Maddy that she wasn't a bit clean. She hadn't thought to change after the arrest.

Bother. Did jailbirds have an aroma? She rather thought she'd heard of such a thing.

She was probably a bigger threat to the sanitary conditions of Jansson's Café than that mouse, and nowhere near as popular. She shoved the pencils behind her ear, not caring if she missed by a bit. Who had room for seven pencils behind their ears after all?

"I'd hoped to visit with you." Maddy didn't have time to scrub up now.

"Me? Really? Because I'd hoped to talk to you. You were a witness when they found Melvin's body. Tell me what —"

A bit surprised to find herself being interviewed, Maddy decided the best route to interviewing Carrie was to be accommodating.

They talked all the while they went through the smorgasbord line. With a steady stream of insults from Dora sprinkled in, Maddy laid out the entire encounter with Melvin and the constable. Carrie seemed delighted, and Nick paid for Maddy's dinner.

A bit too broke for pride, Maddy thanked them as she ate the great pile of delicious food. Crispy fried chicken, mashed potatoes, and gravy. Tender slices of roast beef, a corn casserole, macaroni salad, coleslaw, and a variety of beans floating in a tart yet sweet white dressing. Carrie called it three-bean salad, but Maddy counted six beans and a few other things, so if Carrie was right, the salad was badly misnamed.

Over warm apple cobbler with ice cream, Maddy explained about her thesis paper — at least the part she was willing to admit — and Carrie agreed to be interviewed and granted full access to the newspaper's archives, conveniently stored in their temporary home at the Melnik Historical Society Museum, just a few doors down from Maddy's building. Maddy also learned Nick was building the new museum in the empty lot a bit farther down Main Street. The museum was run by Bonnie Simpson Manning — Tyler's sister.

Maddy's heart was light and her stomach full when she left Jansson's. Several strangers said good-bye; all of them called her Doc. She'd made a friend — three friends actually, if she counted Nick and Dora. Tallulah seemed pleased with Maddy, too; at least she had when she'd thought Maddy had killed that man. Of course, if Carrie or anyone from Melnik knew the truth about her thesis, they'd no doubt chase her out of the village with torches and pitchforks. But for now, Maddy enjoyed the human contact.

Her dinner companions climbed in their cars and drove away. No doubt they had nearly a block to go. She walked the half block to her building, waving at the lonely vampire again. She'd learned that her building, combined with Tyler's, had at one time been an opera house. It had stood decaying for decades until Nick O'Connor had refurbished it and Joe Manning had bought it to rent out. The first floor had twenty-foot ceilings. Other than that, nothing about its present condition hinted at its origins. Maddy didn't care. She unlocked her front door and stepped inside. When the door swung shut, with the dead bolt firmly in place, she should have felt safe.

Instead, she felt like she'd just locked herself in with the ghosts of Melvin Melnik and long-dead opera singers of yore.

The floor overhead creaked.

It was an old building. Of course it creaked.

Good heavens, it was to be expected. Feeling complete empathy for the lonely vampire, she trudged toward the stairway.

She had to go up there, where the creaks were, right next to the door where Melvin had lain dead. Then inflate her mattress and sleep.

Good luck.

"I cannot believe my bad luck."

Tyler shoved his fingers into his hair in frustration. "What did I do to make you drag me into this mess?"

"You're handy, and Hal can't help. He's a suspect." Junior pulled into his reserved parking slot in front of the police station. It was the only car on the block.

"Oh, he's no more of a suspect than I am. Hal wouldn't do a thing like this."

"Well, honestly, you oughta be a suspect, too. The dead body was in your building."

Rolling his eyes, Tyler went back to making his case for being acquitted of his sentence — one zillion hours of community service helping Cousin Junior with this stupid case.

He'd probably get a lighter sentence if he'd actually committed the crime.

"And Steve's got to work at the de-hy plant overnight. Summer's their busy season."

The factory, three miles out of town, dehydrated hay and made it into feed pellets. It was one of the area's best seasonal employers. It took a dozen men to run the big alfalfa choppers, hauling hay to the plant and dumping it, then going back to a new field for more.

"I know that. I worked there a couple summers in high school. But I'm the court-appointed defense attorney for Maddy, if you'll remember. I can't help you question people. It's a conflict of interest. It's unethical. It's illegal. And besides, I need to take over with the boys. Bonnie's gotta be tired of babysitting them by now."

Junior swung his cruiser door open — Tyler had been as good as arrested by his own cousin. "Bonnie's fine. She's better with them than you are."

Tyler knew that for the honest truth, and it hurt his feelings. "Bon-Bon's gonna make a great mom."

"And you're not the defense attorney. You got the doc off, and now you're out of a job. So you might as well help me. You're being paid to act as Melnik's legal counsel."

Tyler glared. "*Paid* is a strong word. I haven't seen a cent yet."

"We can't afford much and you know it, so stop whining."

Tyler reflected on all the high-powered corporate types he'd done legal work for in Omaha. Not a single one of them had ever told him to quit whining.

Home — gotta love it.

Hard to get respect from a guy who'd been the high school star athlete and homecoming king when Tyler was in diapers. Cousin Junior was Tyler's second cousin. Junior's father was a first cousin to Tyler's mom. They'd called the elder Hammerstad Uncle Junior. The whole town had called Uncle Junior's father Grandpa Junior, including Tyler, and Grandpa Junior had, in fact, been Tyler's great-uncle — Tyler wondered what they'd called Grandpa Junior before he had grandkids.

When Tyler's folks had died, Cousin Junior's wife had been a real solid help to Bonnie. She and Junior probably would have taken the family in if Bonnie hadn't been so strong and determined to care for her family.

And Tyler had abandoned her for Liza.

It made him sick every time he thought of it.

Junior led the way to the Andersons' front porch and knocked despite the handy-dandy bell. Helga Anderson, Carrie O'Connor's grandmother, came to the door.

Tyler could never look at Helga without thinking, *It's not over till the fat lady sings.*

The woman needed only a helmet with horns to complete the vision of a Viking wife. Of course, all Tyler's information about Vikings came from reading the *Hagar the Horrible* comic strip in the *Omaha World-Herald*. So what did he know?

Helga started talking before she had the door swung open. "He didn't do it, Junior, and you know it. I won't have you upsetting him."

"Now, Helga —"

"Everybody knows the time of death." Helga turned to her husband, a foot taller and half her width, with half her iron will. "You tell him."

"Twelve to twenty-four hours, right?" Hermann pulled his glasses off and cleaned them with a handkerchief, watching like a hawk for smears while he talked. "Starting at about noon today — that when you found him, Tyler?"

"That's right."

"And the poison had to be administered within twenty-four hours of that."

Tyler didn't even ask how Hermann knew all these details. It was Melnik. Everybody knew. The best thing and the worst thing about a small town was the same thing.

Everybody knew.

If you needed help, lost a job and needed money, had a death in the family, an illness, everybody knew and came to your aid. If you messed up, everybody knew and discussed every detail of the trouble. Tyler wondered what they'd said about Liza. He'd always hoped, because Tyler and his family had never come to Melnik, that no one knew how much she hated them all.

"Well, he was out at the farm all day Sunday, Monday, and today. He's throwing bales for my boy, and his hay was ready on Sunday with rain in the forecast, so they missed church to work."

Hermann Anderson's boy was his daughter's husband, Gus Evans, Carrie's dad, midfifties and still referred to as "my boy." That was one of the things Tyler loved best about Melnik.

"There from sunup to sundown. He came home, and you know baling hay."

Tyler did know baling hay. The kid would have been dead on his feet.

"Sunday night he took a shower, ate about a side of beef, and barely had the energy to wipe the gravy off his chin before he fell asleep. Helga and I were still up when he went to bed. The boy snores like a jackhammer, and he woke me several times in the night. I almost needed the Jaws of Life to pry him out of bed Monday morning, and this morning it was the same thing. Helga fed him and sent him on his way. When he got home, he fell asleep right after a late dinner and went back to his snoring. So he's accounted for all day, every minute of those twelve to twenty-four hours."

"The boy's got adenoid problems," Helga interjected, "but find a doctor who'll take out tonsils and adenoids these days. Didn't hurt any of my kids to have their tonsils yanked out."

Tyler swallowed, glad he'd hung on to his tonsils, just to avoid any yanking.

"And that takes care of the time of death, right? Melvin still alive Monday morning and dead as a carp by midnight, and Kevin's accounted for. I even looked in on him," Junior said.

"You shouldn't have come here." Helga crossed her arms across her ample middle. "He's a good boy, and you'll hurt his feelings by questioning him. We all know Kevin wouldn't do a thing like this."

Junior nodded. "I'd still like to talk to him. I'm sorry, and I believe you, so he's off my suspect list, but Melvin was his uncle. I need to know if the bum ever tried to contact Kevin."

Helga sniffed. "Fine. He's already asleep for tonight. Throwing bales all day again today. Can this wait? Gus is done with his first cutting, so with a good night's sleep, the boy might be less likely to get his feelings hurt."

"I'll come by in the morning. I don't suppose you're planning to have streusel for morning coffee?" Junior grinned. He seemed neither offended by Helga's scolding nor intimidated by it. Tyler was impressed, because he'd dated one of Carrie's older sisters for a few months in high school, and Helga Anderson had scared him to death.

Gus Evans had had a word with him, and so had his wife. But that wasn't enough. The town was lousy with Evanses and Andersons. Hermann had a knack for referring to his hunting rifle collection, casually, no connection between those rifles and the poor soul who might mistreat one of his granddaughters. The man had actually gotten out an old bayonet and shined it while they'd visited.

Tyler had spent the entire two-month relationship looking over his shoulder.

"We'll see. Maybe a good coffee cake will sweeten you up before you injure my boy's feelings."

Junior nodded. "I'll give him a chance to catch up on his sleep, then. Maybe around ten."

Junior scratched in his notebook while he

and Tyler walked back to the car. "Okay, one of my main suspects is off the list."

"So are we done for the night?" Tyler shook his head. "No, of course not. Who am I kidding? You want to go try to get a batch of cinnamon rolls out of Donette and Hal? We could bribe food out of every suspect on the list. I wonder if Shayla can cook. We could track her down in Gillespie if you're hungry. I wanted to take my kids home, but Bonnie told me earlier that if I didn't show up, she'd just keep them overnight."

"Then what were you caterwauling about earlier? You aren't going to see them anyway."

"Yeah, but they wouldn't be staying with her if you hadn't called."

Junior grunted and studied his notebook. "I found a phone number for Shayla. I called earlier and a man answered. He said him and Shayla got married. They ran off and eloped when they found out she was pregnant. He mentioned both of them working at the hospital. He's an orderly, and Shayla's got her LPN and works full-time; she's even got insurance benefits. It sounds like the girl's getting her life together."

"Is Shayla's orderly husband strong

enough to move a body?"

Junior looked up at Tyler. "You're a suspicious man, Tyler." Then a smile bloomed on Junior's face. "I think I'm starting to like you."

Tyler laughed. Junior had always liked him. But Junior liked everybody.

"I think we're done for the night." Junior dropped Tyler off at his car, which was sitting in front of his law office. They both noticed the little rusty wreck of a Toyota sitting beside Tyler's gleaming SUV. And they could see that every light in Maddy's building was on. The woman was spooked, no doubt about it.

"I wonder how the doc is holding up? Is knowing there was a dead body in there giving her night terrors?" Junior gave Tyler a calculating glance. "Checking would be neighborly."

Tyler swung the car door open, reaching for his keys. Nothing. He remembered. He'd given Dr. Snow White his keys, just handed the whole ring over. Law office, house, car. Tyler shook his head. If that wasn't a Freudian slip — arranging another get-together — nothing was.

"I think I will say good night. If she's spooked, she could spend the night at Bonnie's."

Tyler slammed the door in Junior's chuckling face. He stood there until his cousin drove off then approached the good doctor's door.

She had it open before he'd knocked twice. She must have been watching from inside. With two huge front windows, he should have seen her, but the streetlights made a glare that turned the windows opaque. And maybe she hadn't been there waiting. Maybe she'd watched from the upstairs windows and come running.

She'd cleaned up, put on a new set of baggy clothes — black walking shorts and white blouse this time. Bare feet. Her hair was loose, a bit too curly, as if she'd showered, and whatever control over her hair the ponytail had given her was lost.

No pencils.

"Can I come in?"

"Please do." She said it a little too fervently. Her blue eyes flashed gratitude and nerves. "So did you find out anything more about what happened to that man?"

"Melvin Melnik. A lowlife if ever there was one. The man will not be missed. And no, we haven't found out anything."

Swinging the door wide, she whacked herself in the forehead then stumbled back. She had a firm grip on the doorknob, though. Tyler suspected the woman had learned to hang on to something at all times.

Rubbing tomorrow's bruise, she said, "How sad someone would die with that as his epitaph."

Tyler nodded as he passed her. She got too close as she swung the door shut and hit his foot.

"So sorry."

She smelled great. Her smile — well, she looked very happy to see him, and he couldn't imagine he'd made a good impression. So she must be afraid enough that any company was welcome. He couldn't leave her here, he couldn't stay, and he couldn't take her home.

"So how's it going? Does this place go bump in the night?"

"It's a little strange, what with the cadaver. I mean, it's gone but not forgotten, as it were. But I'm fine." She looked sad and less open and friendly than before, completely un-fine.

Tyler wondered what was going on in her head. He'd yelled at her. Told her to stay away from his sons, kicked up a fuss about being her lawyer. She most likely preferred the ghost's company to his.

6

Maddy had never been so happy to see anyone in her life.

She wanted to grab him and hang on. Then she remembered his keys. They made a good-sized lump in her pocket, and when she'd showered in the nasty little bathroom upstairs, she'd laid his keys on her air mattress and noticed there were too many. What looked like a car key with one of those automatic lock and unlock buttons on the key chain, and a few other keys he'd need. She'd noticed his car out front and hoped and prayed he'd stop by. He had to get home, after all.

She'd prayed for a lot of things. The dead man's soul. His family's grief — should there prove to be a family, and in case they grieved. Her own fear of every creaking floorboard. Her shaky financial future. Her work. She'd never lied to anyone, but she certainly hadn't told the whole truth to the good people of Melnik. Did God honor a prayer for her work that included falsehood?

While she pondered and prayed, well, since thinking didn't keep her hands busy after all, she'd curled her hair and put on a bit of makeup — not usual for her at any time, but certainly not before she went to sleep. A certain keyless lawyer stopping by was a definite factor in her decision to primp. Her best black walking shorts. A white blouse she went to pains to keep clean for once.

A spritz of perfume.

And now here he was, and she had no idea what to say. She certainly couldn't keep him here permanently, and his temporary presence, although it allayed her fears for the moment, wasn't going to do so after he left. Which could happen at any moment, especially if she stood here without talking. And so what if he was here for his keys? He was her lawyer. That was all. And a reluctant one at that.

"I saw you and the constable —"

"Junior and I ruled out —"

They both stopped and laughed awkwardly. Maddy noticed her hands were clenched together so tightly her knuckles were white. She wished desperately for something better than a folding chair to offer him. She just had to get some furniture.

"Go ahead." Maddy tore her hands apart and gestured toward the gray metal desk, older and uglier than the constable's, but similarly built. It and the chairs had been in here when she moved. "Why don't we sit down? Tell me about the investigation."

Tyler crossed the echoing room. Each footstep on the bare wood bounced off the four walls and towering ceiling, underscoring to Maddy how big and empty and spooky this building was. He settled in a metal folding chair, and because it was the only other place to sit in the room, she took the equally uncomfortable metal chair behind her desk. Folding her arms on the paper-strewn desktop, she leaned forward. This was almost an interview. Perhaps he'd give her background on Melnik.

"So are your roots deep in Melnik?"

"I'm not going to be part of your anthropology thesis, so don't start."

Maddy had to control a sigh. She masked her frustration. "That's fine. So sorry. Old habit to begin asking questions."

"You mean it's an old habit to treat people like lab rats?"

"Most likely. I'm actually a total bore for the most part."

"No, you're not."

He seemed so sure, Maddy wanted to believe him. But she had years of evidence to the contrary. "Well, thank you. But I spend too much time studying people and not enough befriending them. I had a few people talk to me at the diner, but that was just general chatting. In fact, Carrie O'Connor interviewed me, more than the other way around. I may have my face tucked inside the *Bugle* somewhere next week."

"Are you kidding? You'll be on the front page, above the fold."

"Right next to the deceased Mr. Melnik? Splendid — the whole town will remember I was arrested, and now we'll be linked for all time."

"They'll remember anyway."

"At least there was no mug shot taken of me."

"So are you going to be able to handle this?"

"This?" she asked, knowing full well what he meant.

Tyler just waited.

The silence defeated her. "I'll handle it . . . somehow."

"Creepy, though, huh?"

Maddy nodded.

Tyler seemed to shift the possibilities

around in his head for a long time. At last, looking almost . . . apologetic, he said, "I've got an idea that might help. The boys are at Bonnie's for the night, so they won't notice."

Maddy stiffened. "Notice what?" Was he getting ready to make some smarmy offer to stay with her?

"They won't notice if their dog is gone."

A burst of air escaped her lungs. "A dog?" She was charmed. "You've got a dog that would share my flat for tonight?"

Tyler nodded. "You won't be spooked, but you'll probably be exhausted. He's a puppy, a golden retriever puppy named Riley. I've only been back in town a month. We moved right after school let out. The puppy was the first act of madness after we arrived. He's doing okay on house-training, but he needs to go out at least twice a night, and he'll whine until you take him. He's so hyperactive he makes my boys seem cata-tonic. He's a wiggling, licking, yipping, ADHD dog. But he's really cute. And you won't have a second to think about little creaking floorboards."

Maddy's heart melted. "I'd like that very much. This place is a little eerie at night. I just got to town today."

"I know."

Of course he knew. Could she be any

114

more of a twit? "So the night was stretching long in front of me."

"Can I have my keys?"

The question didn't seem to fit in their conversation. "What?"

"My car keys. I left them with you when I gave you the keys to my office so you could use the phone if you needed to."

"Oh yes, those keys." She was a bit lost in his kindness and his handsome eyes. She didn't move.

"I'll go get him if you give me the keys." Tyler smiled. "You can ride along if you like."

"I'd like that." Maddy leapt to her feet so fast her chair went skidding backward, folded up, and collapsed with a clang of metal on wood. "Very much."

Tyler smiled as Maddy fished for his keys in her pocket. They'd hooked into a dusty handkerchief, and a half-wrapped stick of gum glued the whole mass together. Maddy fought the keys free of her pocket contents.

Looking up, she saw an amused tolerance on Tyler's face, as if her ridiculous clumsiness didn't drive him mad. She had the nearly uncontrollable urge to hurl herself into his arms. Instead, she handed the keys over and they went to pick up her new guard dog.

A few minutes later, with the puppy wiggling in her arms, Tyler drove past Maddy's home. "Let me take you on a brief tour of Melnik."

She couldn't control a sigh of relief. "That would be splendid, thank you."

"That's the statue of Maxie the high school football team created."

Maxie in pads, a helmet, and a uniform. The school colors were gray and white.

The Melnik Mice.

Maddy wondered if they'd ever won a game in their lives.

"And this one was decorated by the VFW."

Maxie in a soldier's uniform, holding a rifle. Maddy thought it looked real. Could the town just leave a rifle lying around like that?

Tyler wound around a corner about three blocks from Maddy's wretched flat. "This is my sister's house."

"Good heavens, who built this thing?"

They slowed and Tyler rolled down a window. Maddy thought she heard the caw of a crow, or maybe a raven — *nevermore.*

"It's awful, isn't it? But it's nice inside. Bonnie and Joe have turned it into a real home. They're going to sandblast the white paint off, and it won't look quite so much like it's dripping blood."

116

"Well, that might help." Maddy was extremely doubtful.

Looking through the large window near the center of the house, Maddy saw Tyler's children sitting beside Joe. He was reading to them.

"You should be with your sons instead of me."

"They like Bonnie more than me." Tyler sounded so glum Maddy wanted to cry for him. "I can't make them behave. I can't even make them like me. My wife was in charge of discipline. I've got a lot to learn."

Maddy didn't comment, but she didn't think the boys had been taught much discipline. No one, not even a child, could so completely forget their teachings. Maddy soothed the sniffling puppy and he settled onto her lap. As she petted him, Riley went to sleep, as relaxed as a baby.

Tyler kept driving, past a mouse in the huge house's front lawn.

"Is this your sister's mouse art contribution?"

A mouse, plain, just sat there. Well, it was on its haunches really. All of the statues were of the same design. The mouse didn't really look like it was sitting so much as it looked for all the world like it was standing up on its hind legs.

"Yeah, she's using her artistic expression to decry the exploitation of the natural world by man." Tyler studied the mouse through narrowed eyes.

"Honestly, that's a lovely sentiment."

"It is, but no one believes her. They think she's just too lazy to fix up her mouse."

"Well, all great artists are misunderstood."

"Yeah, plus when I told her that, she got mad. I try not to upset her in her condition."

Tyler showed her more mice. He was particularly fond of Junior's. Tyler wasn't absolutely sure, but he thought Maxie had on one of Junior's uniforms. Maxie was shorter, but with some hemming of the pants and shirt, Junior wasn't shaped unlike a mouse.

"It strikes me as odd that you've chosen to give me a tour of mouse statues. But I appreciate seeing them. Especially the one outside the day care center dressed like a clown and the one by the nursing home with a walker. That was lovely." In an extremely creepy and shut-down-by-the-health-department kind of way, but Maddy didn't say that out loud.

Tyler took far too long getting her home. Maddy wasn't about to rush him. With the windows open, the cool evening air ruffled

Maddy's hair.

"I can't remember ever being anywhere this quiet."

Maddy had lived in London and Omaha, and she'd done a bit of traveling, but never to a rural area. No cars, no chattering people, no planes overhead or sirens in the distance. Just the silence of people settled into their homes for the night.

Tyler finally pulled up beside her car. "Can you handle it? Bonnie would let you stay with her."

"The puppy will help. I'll make it."

Tyler was out and around the car before Maddy could switch the sleeping puppy around and free a hand to grab the door handle.

He let her out and walked her to her door. It took everything Maddy had in her not to grab him and beg him not to leave her. She might have even done it if she hadn't found him so attractive. A friend she could stay with, but not this handsome man.

"Good night, Maddy." Tyler lingered.

Maddy knew he was worried about her. So she said, "Good night. Thank you for the tour." She turned and boldly went inside her spooky building.

Lying in bed an hour later, with Riley's gentle heartbeat warming her, Maddy decided, even with the dead body and being arrested as sour notes, this was one of the nicest days of her life.

The hammering on her door woke her to full daylight. The puppy licking her face came an instant later. An exhausting night. The puppy wasn't one for long, unbroken sleep. Tyler had in fact lied to her about the little retriever's hyperactivity. He had grossly understated how active the pup was. Still, the baby fuzzball had saved her life . . . or at least her sanity. Her heart tugged at the thought of giving him up.

Sleep dragging at her eyelids, she fought through the cobwebs in her brain and pulled on her clothes in record time. She couldn't answer the door in her nightgown. After all, the whole front of her building was open to the street. She ran downstairs, tripping when she almost stepped on the frolicking puppy. Only her firm hand on the railing saved her. She'd learned to never forgo that.

The knocking continued. It sounded like someone was beating on her door with the side of his fist. She saw Constable Hammerstad at the door, and a twinge of fear surprised her. She'd never feared an officer of the law in her life. Always a law-abiding person, she'd never had so much as a traffic citation or even a warning. Of course, she'd never owned a car in London. The public transportation system suited her.

But in America, she'd acquired a fifteen-year-old Tercel and had been the picture of care behind the wheel.

"I'm coming!" She trotted toward the door, dodged the puppy, and fell forward, close enough to fall against the door and almost brain herself, but her head impacting wood saved her from falling to the floor in a heap, so on balance she was grateful. Twisting at the lock, she saw the flushed anger on the constable's face.

"What happened?"

Constable Junior shouldered past her partially opened door. "Dr. Madeline Stuart, you are under arrest for the murder of Melvin Melnik."

"What? Not again."

Tyler's big car pulled up, his brakes locking. He skidded into the curb and bounced. He was out of the car with the door slammed before the vehicle stopped rocking.

"Sorry, Maddy. I —"

"You have the right to remain silent and I suggest you exercise that right." The constable pulled her wrists behind her, and she heard the metallic snick of the cuffs on her

121

wrists. He stepped up beside her, and she saw the fire of anger in his eyes. "You played me yesterday, and I don't like it. You have the right to an attorney, and here he is."

Junior jerked his thumb at Tyler. "But it's not going so easily for you this time."

"What in the world happened?" Maddy looked at Tyler.

His expression was cool concern. The professional lawyer was back. "I don't know. Junior just phoned and said he was arresting you and to meet you at the police station. But I was driving by and saw this going on."

A crowd gathered, Dora in the forefront. Down the block, Olga Jansson stood outside her diner and wiped her hands on a towel as she stared. The vampire was outside, too. Obviously awake and moving in the sunlight, but no matter how many times Maddy saw him, she couldn't quite remove her suspicion that he was the walking dead.

The hippie lady stepped out, pirouetted, and stared. She was already fitting into Melnik. How early was it? Did these people arise at dawn for fear they'd miss some bit of gossip?

The puppy escaped between Maddy's legs, making her jump sideways and knock her shoulder solidly into the door frame.

Constable Junior caught her arm. Insulting, that. Why, she'd never made one tiny escape attempt in all these hours of their acquaintance.

Tyler snagged the puppy and cuddled the little fellow close to his chest, all the while watching Maddy with those cool eyes. He was her lawyer again, no longer a too-handsome friend with a puppy to share.

Maddy walked to the cruiser. She called up the street, "I'm innocent."

Many in the crowd on the sidewalk nodded and waved. Maddy was unable to return those waves. She hoped they understood and didn't think she was unfriendly.

Junior cupped the back of her head when she lowered herself into the backseat, resigned to another block-and-a-half ride.

7

"C'mon, Junior, couldn't you just ask the woman where she was before you start arresting her? It's embarrassing for her." Tyler unlocked her cuffs.

"And you'll be embarrassed, too, when you have to let her go."

"She goes nowhere until this is confirmed."

Tyler snorted. "And that'll take what? A half hour? She had Riley last night." Tyler held up the squirming puppy. "She could have used some more sleep. You heard her say she'd only been in town a couple of hours before we found Melvin."

The dog started licking Tyler's face. Not enjoying the dog slobber, Tyler set the cute little pest on the floor.

"I didn't ask about the right time." Junior glared at Maddy as if that was her fault.

Tyler crossed his arms and leaned back in his chair.

"Dr. Notchke just phoned and said the body showed signs of being chilled."

Tyler jerked forward. "What?"

"Which means Melvin cooled down a lot faster than he would have otherwise. They're still examining the evidence, but it appears now that he'd only been dead a few hours. And I don't know exactly when she got to town. I'm going to double-check the gas receipts she got when she filled her car in Fremont and see if anyone remembers her."

"I wish you chaps wouldn't speak about me like I'm not here."

Tyler thought she'd been a pretty good sport up to now, but she was looking at the jail cell door as if it had fangs and a healthy appetite.

"I'm sorry." He patted her now-unshackled wrist. "I'll have you out of there faster than we can arrange a bail hearing. The judge works in two counties, so to get bail set, I'd have to go to the next county over from here, which could take half a day — the drive's not bad, but he's hearing court cases, so he's busy. He'll be in this county tomorrow, so if things don't work out with your alibi, I'll arrange bail tomorrow."

"Tomorrow? You mean I might have to spend the night in jail?" She looked down at his feet. Little Riley grinned up at her, wagging his tail. Which Tyler believed was proof positive that the friendly, goofy dog was dumb as a rock. There was nothing to smile about here.

"No, no, of course not. Junior's going to start phoning people right now." Tyler glared at his cousin as he escorted Maddy into the cell.

"Look, this isn't my fault." The poor excuse for a detective swung the door shut with a loud clank. "The doctor said the time of death was sooner. Melvin had her locket in his hand. That gives us a solid piece of evidence and opportunity."

"You said yesterday there was evidence that his hand had been pried open after his death." Maddy clenched the bars like a seasoned felon.

"Dr. Notchke suspects it, but it's not conclusive. His hand was definitely injured postmortem, but maybe you knew he had the locket. Maybe you were trying to get his fist open when you heard Tyler come in downstairs."

"Oh, rubbish." Maddy released the bars and rubbed her arms. Tyler noticed she had goose bumps.

"Are you cold?"

Maddy looked at her arms and back at

him. "No, I'm scared to death I'm going to end up in one of your awful American prisons for killing some man I've never seen nor heard of."

"American prisons aren't so bad."

Maddy made a sound Tyler would expect to come from a wounded, cornered mountain lion.

"Not that you'll ever know that," he added quickly. "You'll be out in no time." Tyler turned to Junior. "You've got no motive. Why would she want to kill Melvin? There's absolutely no link between the two of them."

"A motive might turn up. For one thing, what are the chances some anesthesiologist from England would pick Melnik to write a paper on? Maybe she knew Melvin before."

"I'm an anthropologist, actually."

Tyler ignored her. "Melvin came straight from prison to Melnik and went straight back to prison. Where do you think she met him? On the campus at Oxford?"

"I don't teach at Oxford either. There are other universities in London, you know. Although Oxford is my dream. I hope someday —"

"Like I said, I'm asking questions." Junior got a mule-stubborn look on his face.

Tyler had known his cousin long enough to know arguing with the man at this point would just make him dig in his heels.

Using his best "professional attorney" sneer, Tyler said, "I'd like privacy to confer with my client, please, Officer." Riley tugged at Tyler's shoestrings, and it was hard to keep his professional demeanor intact. He saw Maddy trembling. "Privacy and a sweater. She's freezing."

Junior grunted and slid past Tyler into the narrow hall that ran in front of the two jail cells, one for women, one for men. There was no one in either of them — not counting Maddy — who did count, but not really, because she was innocent.

Why would there be anyone locked up? There was no crime in Melnik.

Tyler thought of Melvin and Gunderson and Wilkie . . . all murdered.

Almost no crime.

Junior left and returned in a second with a gray hoodie sweatshirt with the word HUSKERS printed in huge red letters that stretched all the way across the front and onto the sleeves, dissected by a zipper. Judging by the size, this was Junior's.

"Now I'm going to go search your building for evidence." He handed Maddy the sweatshirt, glared at Tyler, then turned and gave them their privacy, closing the door behind him with a solid thud.

"I did not kill Melvin Melnik."

"I know you didn't." Tyler waved his hand at her then centered a folding chair and sat down. "Now since they've changed the time of death, and you don't have as good an alibi as before —"

"I have a rock-solid alibi. I worked round the clock with my study group up until testing time on Monday. The test went late and my group went out and celebrated the end of the class. I went straight home to sleep in the wee hours. I must have awakened my landlord when I pulled up, because he came and scowled at me and reminded me I had to be out early the next morning. I slept just a few hours then loaded the possessions I hadn't moved here days ago and handed my key to my landlord. If I drove straight here, I'd have still been too late to kill that man."

"Well, borderline."

The look she gave him made him glad there were steel bars between them.

"But as I told you, I didn't drive straight here. I stopped to buy tea at a little shop in Omaha and ended up chatting over oolong and scones for nearly two hours. The owner is the sweetest little British woman, and we've gotten to know each other over the past few months. She'll definitely remember me."

"Do you have a receipt with a credit card record of the time you stopped there? Junior called that shop and there was no answer."

"She's probably closed. She talked a lot about her health. And the tea shop is just something she does for a hobby. If she has a doctor's appointment or something, she just locks up, and she doesn't take credit cards. I paid cash for my tea."

"Well, until we find her, she's not much use as an alibi."

"Then I stopped for gas in Fremont. I used my credit card for that. I don't have that receipt, either, but there will be a record. It will prove —"

"Look, I know. That makes it no longer borderline. You didn't get here until hours after the latest possible time of death. You don't have to convince me, but Junior's insisting on checking with the credit card company. It'll be fine. Like I said, you'll be out in a few minutes."

"And in the meantime, Junior is ransacking my flat looking for a nonexistent connection to that horrible dead man. I think that's shockingly rude."

"Yeah, sorry I couldn't head that off."

"You don't seem like you're all that good

a solicitor, frankly."

Tyler had been mulling the ins and outs of murder, but her highbrow accent and her snippy insult drew his attention and he smiled.

Mistake.

"Nothing about this is remotely amusing."

"Now, Maddy, don't —"

"Get me out of here. Go earn your money."

Tyler rolled his eyes. "Junior will never cough up any cash."

She sniffled.

"Fine, I'll go try to stop him from making a mess in your place."

Her lips quivered. Her eyes closed. For a second, he was sure tears were inevitable. He hunched his shoulders, determined to stay and comfort her.

She swiped one hand over her eyes. "Can you leave the puppy?"

Tyler hesitated. He kept expecting the boys to show up. Eight-months pregnant Bonnie was bound to get tired of chasing them. So far they must be okay, unless they'd killed her and no one had noticed yet.

In Melnik, it was possible.

The boys would notice their dog was missing. But . . . He eased the chubby pup through the bars and Maddy grabbed the little fluffball, sat down on the cot, and pressed warm fur to her cheek.

"I'll go, then. Tell Junior to phone me if you think of anything you need. Junior can take Riley out for a walk, too. Serves him right for arresting you."

"Get out of here." The words were tough, but they lost their intensity when the first tear rolled down her cheek and the puppy licked it away, his feet peddling. The little doofus didn't seem to realize he was in midair instead of running.

Tyler couldn't go. "You know I won't let anything happen to you, Maddy. I'm a good lawyer. Junior's got nothing, and we just have to force him to admit it."

Maddy stood and approached the cell door. Tyler couldn't resist meeting her right across the steel bars. He reached and touched the soft gold of his puppy. His fingers found hers.

"I do appreciate your help, Tyler. I do. I shouldn't have spoken so sharply. I'm so sorry."

Another tear fell. This was so different from Liza's crying. Lots of noise when his wife cried, screaming — sometimes she threw things. She'd even slapped him a few times — more than a few. He'd learned to stay put even though he wanted to run. The storm seemed to pass more quickly if he stayed, and a niggling seed of doubt told him she might turn on the boys, although she never had.

And when had Liza ever, ever apologized?

He couldn't stop himself. The metal bars were magnetized. He was pig iron. He leaned forward. The bars kept them apart except . . . the bars were just wide enough that he could reach her lips with his own.

One healing kiss, a sympathy kiss.

Comfort, reassurance, friendship, support.

Just good manners.

Great manners.

Great kiss.

The dog licked his face and he pulled back. He couldn't go far. She'd reached one arm through the bars and had it wrapped around his neck.

He reached up to help her let go and realized he had his arms through the bars and around her waist. It took some untangling to get away. And that was slowed down by another kiss . . . or two. If the puppy and the jail cell door hadn't been there, he might have kissed her all day. He thought for a few seconds he might anyway.

His brain engaged, and he stumbled back and nearly fell over his folding chair. She backed away from him as if he were a rattlesnake. With one hand over her mouth, she hit the hard cot and sat down abruptly. Riley jumped down and ran out of the cell.

"Please don't leave —"

Tyler didn't think he could.

"— with the puppy."

Oh, the dog, of course.

Tyler returned the mutt. She took him without touching Tyler.

He saw tears welling again, and she buried her face in Riley's thick coat. He was positive Dr. Snow White didn't want him here to watch her cry.

Whether that was his yellow belly talking or not, he ran.

8

"Look at this, Ty."

Junior met him at the door to Dr. Snow's building with a fistful of papers. "Look what she's got planned."

Tyler scowled at Junior. "You didn't need to keep her locked up. You know she didn't kill that bum Melvin Melnik."

Junior slapped him in the chest with the papers. "She's trying to make laughing-stocks out of all of us. Worse than that, she's trying to prove we're a cult or something, worshipping Maxie. If she writes this paper, the whole town will be ruined."

"What are you talking about? Worship?"

"She asked us just yesterday if we worshipped Maxie, remember?"

"Someone is trying to take possession of that rodent you all worship?"

Tyler remembered. He'd called her on it, and she'd backed right off. He looked at the papers, and as he read, he mentally drafted his letter of resignation from her case. He'd turn in his law license before he'd spend any more time with this dishonest, insulting, arrogant little Brit. Tyler refought the whole American Revolution while he read. And America won again.

Junior returned to the stack of papers on her desk. "She wants to prove we're all victims of mass insanity. Her anarchiology paper is going to be about a town that is suffering from delusions and worships an oversized mouse."

"Anthropology." Tyler corrected Junior under his breath. Anthropology, the study of civilizations. Like Margaret Mead, only instead of researching some tribe cut off from the modern world, Dr. Snow White was studying the people of Melnik like they were savages.

"She's got newspaper clippings from the *Bugle,* the *World-Herald,* and one from *Newsweek* from when Carrie got that story printed in there." Junior lifted a flat plastic DVD case. "She's got a copy of the *Current Events* program they did about us."

Tyler well remembered those stirring pieces about how all that was great about America was reflected by Melnik and the citizens' efforts to save their hometown. And that story about Melnik on *Current Events.*

It had happened right when Liza died, so he hadn't seen it air originally, but Bonnie had sent him a DVD of it a couple of months later. Melnik depicted beautifully, full of people who cared and loved each other.

He'd always loved his home, but he'd let Liza convince him Melnik was an embarrassment. The shame of how he'd let her dictate every breath he took still clung to him like a bad odor. And he still had a terrible time making decisions, waiting for Liza to tell him how it was going to be.

Carrie, despite her loathing for mice in general and Maxie in particular, had seen in Melnik the foundations of freedom and ingenuity and dignity that were the backbone of America.

The woman was a wizard with words, and her work had won state and national awards and been widely reprinted. Bonnie had always sent him clippings from the paper, especially ones that mentioned her, and as the museum curator, she'd been featured prominently in any Maxie Mouse news.

Liza wasn't there anymore to ridicule it, as she'd ridiculed everything about Melnik. And without her denigrating opinion influencing him, that paper had lit a fire that had never gone out.

His marriage to Liza had long been over — in his heart — before she died. But vows were sacred, and he'd have kept them all his life. Now with her dead, that story had reminded him of his childhood, his roots. Bonnie and his little brothers he'd so cruelly abandoned. The boys were grown now, no thanks to him. Bonnie had done it all alone.

He'd have never acted on any of those stirrings if Liza hadn't died, killed in a wreck by her own road rage while she was furious at Tyler for driving to Melnik to visit his family.

After her death, Tyler had been too stunned to think clearly. But finally the fog cleared. That DVD came from Bonnie. Carrie's articles reminded him of his love for home. Without Liza there to remind him of Melnik's unworthiness, his desire for home took root. He'd grown up with the safety of knowing everyone by name, and their parents and grandparents and great-grandparents. The experience had shaped him, and he wanted it for his children.

He'd been weak to let Liza alienate him from all that was wonderful about small-town life. He'd been less than a man, less than God wanted him to be. He'd hurt his children, himself, and even Liza by his actions.

For the first time he realized that he'd allowed her to be a tyrant. It had been easier to just take her abuse than to be a man. And he'd been less than a man with his children, allowing them to run wild, calling it sympathy after Liza died, when it was really weakness. Even though she got her way in everything, he now knew Liza had been miserable, and he had to take responsibility for that, at least in part.

The shame stung as he realized another woman held Melnik in contempt. And he'd just kissed her.

He was a fool.

But he didn't have to stay one. "I want off her case."

"No." Junior got all bulled up, his brow lowered, his jaw clenched.

Tyler knew that stubborn look. "I refuse to represent her."

"Too bad. You know her alibi will check out."

"Then why'd you lock her up?" Tyler knew why well enough.

"Because it made me mad when Dr. Notchke changed the time of death and I realized the good doctor could have done it."

"Well, it's not Maddy's fault that Dr. Notchke made you mad." Plus, it was probably an abuse of the office — illegal, and they could be sued.

"True, but I'm glad it happened or I'd have never found her notes about her plans for Melnik."

"So am I." With this evidence of her disdain for Melnik in front of him, Tyler would have arrested her, too, just to let her know how mad he was.

"I realized she could have very carefully planned that killing, knowing full well we'd misjudge the time of death and she'd have an alibi." Junior's excuse sounded like he was practicing his testimony before the judge. "By the time we got done questioning her about this dumb oolong tea she bought, I knew she was innocent. Who makes up a tea flavor like oolong? But arresting her, plus having this building adjacent to the crime scene, gave me probable cause to search this place."

Tyler was momentarily distracted from his anger by the words *probable cause.* Maybe he'd underestimated Junior.

"I want to do this investigation right. I want proof of her alibi before she's released. I never even followed up before. Like a sap, I just took her word for it. But I'm done trusting."

Junior shook a new stack of papers he held

in his hand. "This proves the woman's a skillful liar. I'm doing this by the book. Once her alibi checks out, I'll let her go, and as soon as she's off the suspect list, we can run her out of town on a rail. It looks like she has to do a lot of interviewing to complete this paper. As soon as people realize what she's here for, they'll refuse to work with her. She'll have to move on. Maybe she can go to that town in Kansas with that gigantic ball of twine. Maxie is no different than that."

"This is all confidential, Junior. We can't just go out on the street and tell everyone what we found here." A creak turned Tyler around. He saw Dora staring straight at him; then she whirled and left with a speed that belied her age and weight.

Junior laughed. "Well, that solves that. Consider the word spread."

Tyler had a twinge of pity for poor Dr. Stuart. This town could close ranks like nobody's business. But then he looked down at her handwritten comments on the photocopy of Carrie's beautiful article.

Delusional? Cult? Uneducated? Low intelligence? Inbreeding? Mass insanity?

As if being from Melnik equaled being stupid. As if the people here weren't people of faith who worshipped God, not some oversized mouse.

His pity died, replaced by anger. And that soothed the fear in his heart. Fear mixed with hope, awakened by the pretty, clumsy doctor. Hope that had grown when he'd kissed her and held her in his arms.

Hope. He thought he'd outgrown it, but obviously a spark remained.

Well, he'd just had another growth spurt.

He looked up at Junior's flushed, glowering face. "I want to be there when you unlock that door."

Junior jerked his chin down in a taut nod. "You bring the tar. I'll bring the feathers."

Junior came in and Maddy almost cried.

She'd been here for hours. The constable had been in here only once all day. He'd taken the puppy. She'd asked him questions, but he seemed furious about something and hadn't responded. She wondered what they'd make of her research notes and hoped they didn't look too close. Her project was private, but nothing she was ashamed of. She was light-headed from not eating. Weren't they supposed to feed you in jail?

This morning, Junior had awakened her and brought her straight here. Thank heaven he'd given her a moment in the loo before

142

locking the door. She hadn't eaten all day, and the afternoon was nearly past.

He jerked open her cell with that same suppressed anger and stepped aside. "Your alibi checked out; you're free to go. I recommend you get in your car and start driving."

"What?" She saw Tyler standing in the next room. She hurried toward him until she saw his face.

Rage. Pure and simple.

As she passed through the door, her knees wobbled and she stumbled. Not from her usual lack of grace, but from weakness brought on by hunger mixed with fear. What were they both so angry about? They wouldn't be letting her go if they seriously thought she'd killed that man.

"What's the matter?"

Then she looked past Tyler and saw more people, and more and more. She thought she'd drawn a crowd before, but that was nothing compared to this. Through the open door, she saw the sidewalk was packed, and the street beyond the sidewalk, too.

Tyler leaned close, and she smelled him and remembered that kiss. She'd hardly kissed anyone in her life. She'd been an awkward, bespectacled bookworm with no people skills from birth. Who was going to kiss her? And then Tyler had, and she'd begun to believe something wonderful was happening to her.

She'd felt like a butterfly emerging from a cocoon. Maybe she'd found someone who saw past the worm.

What a joke.

That joy, despite hunger and Junior's anger, had carried her through this awful day in jail. She'd thought Tyler would come and set her free, maybe kiss her again, say lovely words.

Instead, his expression took a fly swatter to her newborn butterfly.

She wanted to run from all the glaring eyes. Get in her car and get out. But she had nowhere, absolutely nowhere to go, and no money to get there.

She stopped. "What is going on? I'm not leaving town, and I'm not budging from this spot until one of you tells me."

She saw Tallulah in the crowd. For once the woman wasn't shouting. But her furious expression said more than words.

Tyler stepped in front of her, his shoulders so broad she couldn't see past him. "I'll tell you what's going on, Dr. Stuart."

"Dr. Stuart?" The contempt lacing his voice made her step back.

"Yes, Dr. Stuart the anthropologist. We found your research papers."

Instantly Maddy knew. They'd searched her building. Of course they'd found her out. She fumbled behind her for the wall and slumped against it and then felt cornered, which she was.

"I . . . I don't know what you think about my research, but there's nothing in it to upset the whole town." Which wasn't true. She'd known they'd be upset, which was why she'd withheld the full truth.

"Don't waste any more time lying."

"L–lying? I didn't lie."

"I read it all, Dr. Stuart."

"You had no right —"

"Junior had a search warrant, and you sent me over there. That's the very definition of the word *right*. The contempt you feel for Melnik. The insults dressed up like scientific research. We worship a mouse instead of God. Where'd you get a stupid idea like that? Is that what passes for education these days?"

"No, I mean the word *worship* isn't . . . I never intended to write a paper questioning your faith, just looking into the . . . somewhat . . . obsessed devotion to your town's —"

"Idol? Fertility god? Your words. Do you think we believe Maxie has some supernatural power?"

"No, of course not!"

"Well, that's not what your research paper says."

"You're quoting a list of questions I found interesting. I intended to study all aspects of your town. Just because I said it doesn't mean I believed it."

"Well, if believing what you say isn't a requirement, then you can say any insulting thing you want, can't you? But what you can't say to us right now is that you cared one bit if your scientific research would damage this town."

"Damage the town? How could I —"

"We've got companies" — he cut her off — "considering us for small factories that would bring good jobs. We've got young people who have picked Melnik to call home, even though they commute to bigger towns to work and have to drive through four other small towns to get to Fremont and five small towns to get to Sioux City. The school has grown, our tax base has grown, the business district is being revital-ized. A nasty little smear piece like your research paper would destroy all of that. But you don't care because you don't care about us." He leaned down until his nose almost touched hers. "None of us."

He meant, *You don't care about me.* And

that was absolutely, patently untrue. She cared about him so much it scared her all the way down to her two left feet. Two minutes ago it had thrilled her. But now she saw that her caring was only going to hurt.

She looked down. She'd done it again.

The worst ever.

As always, she'd alienated people. Her career was ruined if the paper wasn't written. Her future looked bleak. Her heart was quite possibly broken. And worst of all, when he put it this way, she knew Tyler was right. It was a stupid, insulting paper that didn't begin to rise to the level of serious research. A paper that, if she'd have written it and promoted it as she'd planned, would glorify and enrich her while hurting the people of Melnik.

Which meant that God was disgusted with her, too.

And she deserved all of this.

She looked up, her eyes locked on Tyler; then she scanned other faces, surprised how many were familiar after one day in town. And she told them the total and utter truth. "You've made your point. I didn't consider the harm that could be done to your town when I decided to write my paper. So I agree to drop the thesis." Which meant she'd drop her chance at a second PhD and her chance at a job.

None of the faces in the crowd softened. Which made it harder to tell them this next thing. "I can't leave town until September. I've got nowhere else to go. I'm so sorry."

Those words, those stupid, stupid apologies. She was so sick of uttering them with every clumsy step she took and every insulting word she spoke. She was smart. She had the paperwork to prove it. But what good were book smarts if you lived your life like a fool?

God, forgive me. Please. Please. Please.

And she knew instantly that He did, because He always had. God was her resting place. The only one she'd ever found. The only friend she'd never alienated.

Only God had enough patience and love to abide Dr. Madeline Stuart.

She threaded her way through the crowd. No one accosted her, although she feared they might. The street was packed all the way to the corner. She slid this way and that to get through, although mostly they moved back to let her pass, as if touching her would infect them with something.

She came face-to-face with the strange man with no teeth. She sidestepped.

He blocked her, glaring as if she'd personally insulted him. "I moved to this town because everyone made it sound so nice. I should have never come. Your paper's gonna ruin everything."

"I'm not going to write it. I promise." She raised her voice. "I promise."

No one responded, and she went around the man, though he moved so his shoulder bumped hers hard enough that she staggered.

No one else interfered with her progress, though.

Once she'd passed them all, she walked swiftly toward her home for the next three months. She'd paid the rent for June, July, and August. She owned a nonrefundable plane ticket home dated for early September. Beyond that, she had about two hundred dollars in her bank account and a student visa that made it illegal to get a job.

She couldn't afford to go elsewhere. She stopped at her door and looked back. The townsfolk had rounded the corner to watch her, but they were also talking among themselves. Tyler was toward the back of the crowd, but she picked him out without a second's effort. His anger pinged like a sonar beacon, bouncing off her, warning her away.

She turned and entered her building.

Just another prison.

9

Junior came into the diner and sat down across from Tyler in the vinyl booth. "The boys okay?"

Tyler nodded. "I can't get them away from Bonnie. I thought we'd gotten past some of the old problems resulting from Liza's death. The boys had to get used to me being in charge because Liza was the disciplinarian in the family." A disciplinarian who never disciplined the boys and never let up on him. The boys still treated him with the contempt they'd learned from their mother.

"But they've taken to Bonnie and they're crazy for Joe. That guy is a genius with kids."

"Yeah, Jeffie Piperson is his best friend."

"Jeffie is hanging around Joe? So that means Jeffie is hanging around my boys?" Tyler's heart started pounding with fear.

Junior waved his hand at Tyler, brushing aside his worries. Yeah, right, the words *Jeffie* and *worry* were synonyms in Melnik.

"Bonnie said Joe's almost earned a teacher's certificate. The kids' favorite elementary school teacher retires next year and they've already offered Joe the job. He'll be perfect for it."

"So he might be my boys' teacher. And Bonnie's as good as become their mother." Tyler sighed. "I don't know if I can talk them into coming home. They were with me, or rather I was with them, all afternoon. I sat with them at the swimming pool."

And they now insisted on being called Ben and Johnny, which Tyler had to force himself to do. He could hear Liza slicing him to bits every time he didn't say their full names.

"They're staying the night with Bonnie again. I may have to move in to spend time with them." Tyler said it with a smile, but it was the truth, and there was nothing funny about it.

"You'll work it out." Junior leaned forward a bit and spoke quietly, which Tyler found ludicrous, because Dora was in Jansson's and she had ears like a bat — a bat with long-range, high-tech eavesdropping equipment. "I finally caught up with Shayla. I think she's ducking me, which doesn't look good. But I asked the Gillespie police to watch her place, and they saw her come home about ten minutes ago. They picked her up. Want to ride over with me?"

Tyler shrugged. "Sure, it beats my empty house."

"I'm doing background checks on a few other newcomers in town to see if they have any connection to Melvin. Luna Moonbeam has a few minor arrests for drug possession."

"Who?"

"The new antiques dealer. I'm waiting for more details. Melvin went to prison for arson, but he had some drug involvement, so they could be connected somehow."

"And Dolph Torkel, the vampire guy, a few weird things there, but no crimes."

"Weird how?"

"Well, he's real quiet about himself. And he comes and goes at odd hours, sometimes for days at a time, and no one knows where he goes."

Tyler grimaced. "So he visits his mother and guards his privacy. There's no crime there."

Junior snorted as he consulted his notes. "The plumber, Jamie Bobby Wicksner, had to come from a hard background to have teeth like that. I haven't dug up much on him yet."

"I don't think you can seriously suspect a

man just because he has poor dental hygiene."

Junior shrugged. "You know, having a bunch of new folks in town has made my job a lot harder. We probably need a larger police force. The city has to be making more money with the property taxes on new houses and the refurbished Main Street buildings. They could at least make Hal and Steve full-time, maybe pay for some good training programs."

They debated crime and punishment in Melnik all the way to Gillespie, but they had to quit once they picked up a very pregnant — and very cranky — Shayla from the police station. Tyler had never met the girl before, but he'd known Wilkie and Rosie Melnik, Shayla's parents, and Shayla favored her father. Lank dishwater blond hair, blue eyes, bad attitude.

A perfect next-generation Melnik.

Her husband had been called and was on his way to the police station. Cell phones worked in Gillespie, and the police promised to contact him and redirect him to Melnik.

Tyler and Junior drove Shayla back to Junior's office. The girl was so sullen, Tyler expected Junior to toss her in jail just for annoying him.

"Where were you from midnight Sunday

till Tuesday morning?"

She scowled at them. "I don't have to talk to you."

"No, you don't. You can get a lawyer and have him present for questioning. But I'm locking you up until the lawyer gets here. Hunting for you all day just wore my patience clear to the nub. It's enough to make you a suspect, and I can arrest you and hold you for up to forty-eight hours, waiting till a lawyer can sit in on questioning. I'm not letting you walk out till I get some answers."

"I was home in bed from midnight to six Monday morning. I had the early shift at the hospital and had to be there by seven. I worked all day. My husband was home, and we stayed up pretty late Monday night, nearly until midnight, I'd guess. He'll vouch for me."

"I can check the time sheets at the hospital, but that leaves midnight Sunday to Monday at 6:00 a.m."

"I'm a married woman. My husband was with me." Shayla ran her hand over her rounded belly. She wasn't as far along as Bonnie, but the young woman was very definitely expecting.

"He was asleep." Junior shook his head. "Not good enough. Did you get any phone calls, wake up in the night and log on to your computer? Anything?"

Shayla shook her head. "I didn't even know Uncle Melvin was alive until he turned up here and killed Gunderson. Then they locked him up about an hour after people found out he was in town, when he set Bonnie and Joe's house on fire. Why would I care about him?"

"Because he was fighting for a share of the money you got when your dad died and the town repossessed Gunderson's property. That's money Melvin would have taken from you, Kevin, Donette's baby, and Hal. You'd have had to pony up your share, and you've already spent it. The courts could have garnished your wages. Plus, you've got a history of killing people."

Shayla leaned forward and pounded a fist on Junior's desk. "I've never killed anyone."

"Not for lack of trying."

"As for that money, Melvin should have been suing Joe. Suing me would have been a waste of time. Squeezing blood out of a turnip. We should have gotten more." Shayla clenched her fists. "Gunderson was rich. You took away the property his family had stolen from mine but none of the money they'd earned on it. We should have split up everything he had."

"Don't start this again." Junior waved his

hands in disgust. "The court decided that, not me, and you got plenty."

"Mine's all gone. Joe's still rich."

"That's because you blew yours and Joe saved his. No one's fault but yours. And all this mad tells me you've got a motive for killing your uncle, and since you poisoned your father, who you lived with all your life, I don't think you'd hesitate long before poisoning an uncle you've never met."

"But knowing Dad is what made me want to kill him, and that was a spur-of-the-moment thing. I'd have never pre . . . premed . . . premmy-tate . . ."

"Premeditated?" Tyler supplied.

"Planned ahead on a thing like that." Shayla gave Tyler a sneering look that said, *Don't call me stupid.*

Note to self: Don't make the little killerette mad.

The phone rang, late in the evening though it was. Junior listened, then, covering the mouthpiece of the receiver, said, "It's the coroner."

He listened intently, grunting on occasion, then began scribbling in his notebook.

"Thanks, Doc. Appreciate it." Junior hung up. "They did thorough testing on the poison. It's definitely antifreeze that killed him, but there's one problem."

Tyler seriously doubted there was only one.

"Turns out antifreeze isn't poisonous."

"Then how'd it kill him?" Tyler tried to fit that piece of information into this mess.

"Modern antifreeze isn't poisonous. Someone gave him an old formula. And the doctor said the change in antifreeze's makeup was made awhile ago. It's getting hard to find the old stuff."

Junior stared at Shayla.

"Don't look at me. My dad brought that stuff home to use on my cat. I don't know where he got it."

A loud rap at the door turned Tyler around. A hulking man turned the knob and came in partway, holding the door open.

"Can Shayla leave yet? I'm telling you, she was with me all night."

Junior rolled his eyes. "You were asleep."

"Hi, honey." Shayla turned and smiled at her husband.

Tyler saw genuine affection in Shayla's cold little eyes.

"Take her. We're done here." He jabbed his pencil eraser at Shayla. "But the next time I want to talk to you, you get over here. It makes you look guilty to hide from me the way you did today."

"Whatever." Shayla flounced out.

When they'd exited the building, Tyler asked, "Are you sure you should have done that?"

Junior's eyes hardened and he tucked the pencil and notepad in his pocket. "I didn't tell you everything."

Tyler sat up straight.

"You know how the coroner told me the body had been chilled to hide the time of death?"

"Yeah."

"Well, turns out he was chilled, but before that he was heated up."

"What?" Tyler felt his brows arch to his hairline.

"Yep. Someone was messing around with the time of death."

"But wouldn't those two things offset each other?"

"Not necessarily. It took a lot of testing to figure out there was cell damage indicating a fairly warm heat was applied to the body for about twenty-four hours; then the body was chilled for just a few hours. The coroner tried to explain it to me, but honest, I couldn't understand much of it. I hope she explains it better to a jury."

"So when did he die?"

"About two days before Doc Stuart moved to town."

"Two days — but wasn't that when . . ."

"That was twenty-four hours after she was in town for a day, leaving off her stuff. And antifreeze takes awhile to kill, up to twenty-four hours. She's back at the top of our suspect list."

Tyler felt such hot satisfaction at the thought of locking up that Melnik-destroying snob, he knew he shouldn't even be involved with this. He also knew he wouldn't be this furious with Dr. Snow if she weren't so beautiful, and if he didn't enjoy rescuing her all the time, and if she hadn't tempted him to forget about swearing off women. He needed revenge for that even more than he did for her character assassination of Melnik.

"But what about the old antifreeze?"

"I quit searching her building after I found those papers. That building has stored a lot of stuff over the years, including supplies for the mechanic who used to rent the building just behind it. Wanna bet there's some old antifreeze in the basement?"

Tyler wouldn't take that bet even if he was a gambling man. Which he wasn't. He'd found marriage enough of a risk. He'd never been tempted to add slot machines.

"You're back on as her lawyer."

Tyler shook his head. "I'll quit. I'll renounce my law license."

"Well, that'll take awhile. Surely you've gotta file papers to do that. Until you get notice you're disbarred, you're either her lawyer or her cellmate. I'll lock you up, and I can make the charges stick. You'll really lose your law license then. You'll lose custody of the boys, probably do some real time in jail, be publicly disgraced and penniless before I'm done with you. You pick."

Tyler sat frozen in his chair.

Junior rounded his desk and held the door open for Tyler.

Tyler didn't move.

"Well?"

"You told me to pick. I'm still thinking!"

"I can't arrest her alone. I want to wring her neck too bad. Get up."

"I'd perjure myself if you did, cover for you."

Junior chuckled and jerked his head toward his car. "And this time I'm not letting her go. I'm personally giving her a life sentence just because this case is so aggravating. And if Dr. Notchke doesn't quit changing the time of death, I'm throwing her in, too."

"You've got no grounds to hold Maddy, Junior."

"There you go, being her lawyer. Can't

160

control yourself. And I do have grounds. She's a flight risk, and the way this thing keeps coming back around to her, this time, I'm convinced she did it."

"She's not a flight risk. For Pete's sake, she's penniless. Flight costs money. You heard her — she can't even leave town."

"Well, she's an accomplished liar. She proved that in spades with that stupid Maxie paper. So she just might have some money socked away, too. I'm holding on to her. Now come on. She might have already skipped town and hopped a plane for England. Then we'd have to extradite her." Junior froze.

Dr. Snow might indeed have flown the coop. The hurt caught Tyler by surprise, which made him plow into Junior's broad back when Junior stopped suddenly. "What now?"

"The closest I've ever come to extraditing someone is calling the Gillespie police to watch out for Shayla. This is a big case for me." Junior turned, looking worried. "You think extraditing people is expensive? I'm on a limited budget."

Tyler shrugged. "Probably. At least I'll bet you have to pay to fly her back."

"I say if she left the country, we just let her go." Junior scratched his chin.

"Might as well. This is Melvin Melnik after all. It's not like she killed anyone important." Tyler flinched when he heard himself say that.

Junior furrowed his brow in pain from thinking. "Well, we can decide that if she's gone. C'mon."

Tyler's hunger for revenge overwhelmed his desire to avoid Maddy. "Fine, but this time, I'm slapping on the cuffs."

Junior nodded as Tyler passed him. "Deal. But that'll come back to haunt you on appeal."

Tyler stepped into Junior's car and had to fight the urge to turn on the siren so everyone in town would come and see what was going on.

10

"What is going on?"

The pounding broke into her tortured thoughts. No puppy to get through this night. Her house was creaking like a whole family of ghosts lived in the walls. Maddy was tucked in bed. Well, *tucked* was a little strong. She was lying on her inflatable mattress, tormenting herself for being such a twit and insulting all these nice people with her idiotic theory about worshipping a mouse.

Where had she ever gotten the notion this would make a good paper?

Of course, just studying small-town life had merit. But that would never land her on *Oprah*. Which meant her motives had been purely selfish, which made her a twit for insulting all these nice people with her idiotic theory about worshipping a mouse, which meant her motives had been purely selfish, which made her a twit for insulting all these nice people with her idiotic theory about worshipping a mouse, which meant her motives had been . . . The circling of her thoughts was driving her mad, until she wanted to bang her head against something really hard.

And then the fist on her door had interrupted the torment.

The pounding was so familiar that she took the time to dress before she ran downstairs. She wanted to be comfortable in her cell.

Junior and Tyler glared at her as she swung the door open.

"Dr. Madeline Stuart . . ."

Maddy ignored the rest and just turned her back with her hands behind her. "What happened this time?"

The cuffs clicked on. Maddy noticed the touch and the familiar scent, and she glanced behind her back to see Tyler doing the honors.

Her feelings were hurt, but she did her best not to show it. "You know, you really shouldn't do this and then pretend to be my lawyer. Any case they bring against me will collapse on appeal."

Tyler smirked. "I'll risk it, Dr. Stuart."

He took her arm and led her to the cruiser.

"You both know I didn't kill that man.

You know it. I've got no motive. I've got no means. What poison do I have? And you just found out my alibi clears me for the time of death. So I've got no opportunity." Maddy was rather proud of herself for remembering all three. "Why on earth are you arresting me this time?"

"The time of death has changed, and we think we've got means, too." Tyler opened the back door of the squad car. "The basement of this building you rented is a strong possible source of the very unusual and specific poison used to kill Melvin."

"You changed the time of death again?" Maddy looked over her shoulder and glared. "Can't you people ever settle on anything?"

Tyler shielded her head as she lowered herself into the car. She looked back at him. "You don't need to worry about my head. I'm getting good at it." She tried to shake off his hand and whacked her skull on the door frame.

Tyler's hand slipped, catching a bit of her hair between his fingers. She kept glaring, but his eyes changed. His fingers caressed her disheveled head. Gentle now, too gentle. His eyes focused on his hand in her hair. He looked enthralled for a second; then his expression turned to stone.

Maddy could read his mind. He liked the

165

way her hair felt. And he blamed her for that. This all had more to do with the disturbing effect they had on each other than her perceived character assassination of Maxie Mouse or Tyler's belief that she was a killer.

"So whatever the new time of death is, I'll probably have been working then, too. I've been very, very busy. For a long time. And you still have absolutely no motive. Why would I kill a man I've never met?"

Tyler stared down as she settled in the backseat of the squad car. Then his eyes brightened. He snapped his fingers. "How about Melvin was snooping around in your stuff and figured out what you intended for your thesis? What if you knew he'd ruin your chance of getting your project finished? You've already admitted you're broke and need to finish this paper desperately. I wonder just how desperate you are."

Maddy's heart broke as she stared at him. He looked so pleased with his warped reasoning. That heartache, more than any-thing, proved to her that she'd begun falling in love with the big dummy. She shook her head and stared straight out the front wind-shield.

"I didn't kill Melvin Melnik. Take me to jail, Junior. I don't wish to have an attorney provided for me. I'll just wait until sanity prevails and you have to let me go."

"That won't be anytime soon," Tyler muttered.

"That sanity prevails in this town? Now why doesn't that surprise me?"

Tyler slammed the door and got in the front seat.

And that hurt, too.

He'd always ridden in the back with her. Getting arrested and riding to jail was the closest they'd come to a date.

And she was such a dimwit that she deserved to go to jail. Actually, that cot was more comfortable than her inflatable mattress, anyway. And no dead men had been near it . . . at least none that she knew of.

They pulled up in front of Junior's office. "Don't you Americans ever walk anywhere?"

Remembering that she'd been left for the duration before, she managed to talk them into unshackling her and letting her have a minute in the loo.

She looked at the idiot who had kissed her through the cell bars so gently just hours ago and who now escorted her to her cell. Wanting to remind him of how stupid they'd both been, she narrowed her eyes at him and blew him a kiss through the bars.

She didn't even flinch when the cell doors clanged shut. The noise was so familiar she'd come to think of it almost like an art form.

Heavy metal music.

"Hear that, Tyler? They're playing our song."

Tyler actually convinced the boys to come with him the next morning.

He knew he needed to go consult with his client, but Junior was running down all her alibis and that'd take awhile, so Tyler gave himself the morning off. Sure, he could have rushed in there with bail money. And he could have strong-armed Junior and probably gotten Dr. Snow out. But he didn't.

No way.

He and the boys turned their attention to cleaning the upstairs of his building. Which meant he cleaned and they ransacked. He walked down to the city office and arranged for a Dumpster to be set outside his alley window so he could drop stuff two floors down into it. His boys were looking forward to that.

He started sorting and the boys ran wild. Once the Dumpster arrived, they discovered they enjoyed listening to stuff crash, so they actually were some help.

Junior interrupted him around noon. "I've got the information on your client, as if you care."

Ben careened into one of the tall cupboards. Tyler held his breath and realized he should have checked them all for bodies before he let the boys in here. The cupboard door swung open, full of garbage, but corpse-wise, it was clear.

"What have you got?"

Junior pulled out his notebook. "She's got an alibi, but it's thin. She admits to being in town last Saturday for about three hours. I've got fairly solid evidence to support that. Dora saw her, of course, although the old battle-ax worried she'd help clear Dr. Stuart if she told me. Still, she couldn't control her urge to blab, so she admitted she'd seen the doc come, unpack, disappear inside for a long time, then drive away."

Tyler read the notes. "So Maddy was here Saturday morning. When did Melvin die?"

"The coroner — that Dr. Notchke is a testy woman, by the way; I'm not the one who keeps changing the time of death — suspects now that Melvin gave up the ghost late afternoon on Sunday. She won't officially narrow it down past a twenty-four hour window, noon Sunday to noon Monday."

"And is that about how fast the antifreeze works? So Maddy could have dosed him with it Saturday?" Tyler pictured Maddy offering a deadly cocktail to Melvin. For some reason, Tyler pictured her in a slinky red evening gown, long slit up the thigh, low-cut, a cigarette holder about a foot long in her hand. She'd brush up against Melvin with a martini glass — tinged bright blue with antifreeze.

Mata Hari with a doctorate.

It made him sick to think of it. No way she killed anybody. She'd have dumped the drink down her red dress before she got him poisoned. "She'd have been out of town, safely surrounded by other students, before he died."

"Yeah, except it works faster than that when it's given in a strong dose, and Melvin's was strong. The doctor said so."

"Wait a minute — which doctor?"

"Dr. Notchke. This case is just lousy with doctors and lawyers, isn't it?"

"Hey! Leave me out of this."

"Dr. Notchke said, based on the content of Melvin's stomach, he'd been given too strong a dose to take that long killing him. If she'd given it to him Saturday morning, he'd have died before Sunday noon. The coroner thinks Melvin must have been

170

poisoned late Saturday night, possibly even early Sunday morning, for the poison to kill him when it did, and Dr. Stuart has a rock-solid alibi from Saturday afternoon at two until she showed up here Tuesday."

Tyler pointed at one of Junior's notes. "She was in another all-day, all-night cram session with five other people."

Junior nodded. "The students even commented on her taking off Saturday morning. Her landlord wanted the place cleared out about the same time her class final was done. She had two carloads of her possessions. So she had to haul that stuff up here, go back, and repack her car. She was studying until her Monday evening test. She slept in her stripped apartment Monday night and took off for Melnik Tuesday morning."

"So you have to let her go again?"

"It's close. The coroner is sure it was a stiff dose of poison, but what if she's wrong? Or what if Melvin did something to delay the effects? Alcohol can alter the effects of medicine and poison. Maybe it slowed down Melvin's reaction."

"Did Dr. Notchke say it was possible?"

"No."

"You're reaching. She's innocent." Tyler sighed with relief and then felt guilty. He didn't want to be rooting for the sneaky little anthropologist. But then, just because he hated her didn't mean he wanted her to go to jail for a crime she didn't commit.

Well, maybe a few years wouldn't hurt her.

Junior got that mule-stubborn look on his face. "Letting her go and arresting her again is getting embarrassing. Let's go search her basement for the antifreeze first."

"Junior, she's innocent. You can't keep her locked up just because you're embarrassed."

"Why not? That's the best part of being sheriff."

"It's not even that embarrassing. The town likes to see her arrested. If you need to haul her in a fourth time, no one will give you a hard time."

"I suppose you're right. And she didn't do it, which makes me inclined to let her out." Junior mulled over his notes and then looked up at Tyler. "So who do you think did?"

Tyler shrugged. "That's your job. I've got an old building to clean."

Johnny fell against a box of papers, which exploded. The boy rolled into another old cupboard.

"You oughta go through this place for dead guys before you let the boys play up here." Junior slapped his notebook shut and went downstairs, grumbling.

11

"Next time just phone, okay? No need to drive over and arrest me. I'll walk over. And I didn't need a ride home, either."

Tyler couldn't hear Junior's deep voice respond, but he must have agreed to unarrest Dr. Snow, because he heard the front door to Maddy's building slam. Even the slam sounded sarcastic. He hoped she'd just leave him alone. Write her stupid paper and leave town.

Her feet pounded on her stairway. His stomach sank even before she shoved open the door to his building. He stepped out of the kill zone — a good thing, because she would have nailed him with the door. Just like their first meeting.

A tale to tell their grandchildren.

Tyler about choked on that thought.

"And as for you . . ." She was beautiful, a fuming, dangerous, hair-triggered fairy-tale princess with him in her sights. He hated

173

how much he wanted to go calm her down, cheer her up, kiss her out of her rage. It occurred to him that he had never, never, ever, not for one single split microsecond in all their years of marriage, been interested in teasing Liza out of a bad mood.

Or brave enough to try if he had thought of it.

She's a sneak, a liar. She hates your hometown. Liza hated Melnik. Remember Liza.

He was a bona fide idiot, and no wall of framed diplomas and degrees could convince him otherwise. He took a step toward her but she was charging, so he barely moved before she had her nose stuck right up to his.

The boys had tried her door a thousand times this morning and it was locked tight. When they saw her come in, they whooped and raced for the opening like a pair of hogs heading for a hole in the fence. Ben tripped over a box and sent it tumbling, almost knocking Tyler on his backside. Bowling for Fathers. The sport of his kids.

"Are you about done arresting me?" Her hands were fisted at her side, but Tyler knew she'd never throw a fist.

She hates Melnik. Remember that.

"Look, I know you didn't kill Melvin. I've known that from the first second I saw you.

But the evidence has pointed to you three times. We have to look into it."

"You're my lawyer. You're supposed to be on my side."

Oh, he was on her side.

Stupid, stupid, stupid. Remember why she's wrong, wrong, wrong for you, stupid.

She calmed down — not all the way down, but enough to confirm his theory that she wasn't going to pound on him. She jabbed him in the chest. "I am not going to write that paper."

Okay, she just took away a huge part of the reason to avoid her. Still, she hated the town.

"I love this town." Her voice broke. She squared her shoulders and went on. "It breaks my heart that no one likes me anymore. They were all so kind. I've always been such a clumsy oaf around people, and for the first time, even after only a day here, I thought I could find friends, not be a pariah."

Another big reason gone, but not the biggest one. You barely know her, and you married Liza too fast. And you're a moron about women.

"I am such a moron about people." She slung her arms straight out at her sides and

175

almost nailed him when she spun away to pace.

Tyler ducked then braced himself to save her. Her hands and feet really should be registered as lethal weapons — at least lethal to herself.

She'd never throw a punch, but she might manage to kill him by accident.

"If I had written that paper, I would have hurt your fair city, and because my idea was so ludicrous, I'd have also been the laughingstock of the academic world. But no one in this town will ever believe me."

She kicked a stack of paper into the air as she stumbled along. "If they'd forgive me, I might be able to get approval for a new topic. I'd write a simple study of life in a small town. It wouldn't be groundbreaking, but it would be a legitimate thesis, and it could earn me my degree."

She whirled back toward Tyler and took his hand, her eyes big and deep and shining blue against her milky white skin. "Could you help me, Tyler? Everyone loves you. They'd trust you, and I'd promise to let them all see the paper, every word, before I sent it in. I'd even let them watch me put it in the envelope and mail it."

She hugged his hand, held in both of hers to her chest, practically tucked under her chin. The woman was begging. She was so beautiful when she begged.

Tyler had been thinking about something important, but when her hand touched his, he forgot everything except how sweet and clumsy she was and how kindhearted, and the way her eyes filled with tears and how she said, "So sorry," every single time she almost killed someone.

She'd come in here furious, and she couldn't even sustain that. She'd turned her wrath on herself before he'd had time to resent her temper. He even figured out why she was so clumsy. Her mind was working at a hundred miles an hour because she was such a genius — book smart, not people smart, but even the things she did badly completely occupied her mind. Not leaving her time to watch where she was going.

He got lost in those pleading eyes for a second too long. She must have taken his silence for a no — better than taking it for him being mesmerized — because her chin dropped, her shoulders slumped, her pants slipped low on her hips. "I don't blame you." She turned away.

"Yeah, I'll help you."

She whirled around, her eyes on fire with excitement and intelligence and hope and something warm and alluring. But happy or not, she was still a klutz. She tripped on today's pair of baggy pants, the same ones she'd been arrested in, and fell over backward.

He'd known her two whole days. He thought he was ready. He grabbed, but she even fumbled that. They both went flying over.

She grunted as she landed smack on top of him. Papers exploded into the air then began raining down on their heads.

"You'll really help me?" She rolled off him. "I'd be so grateful."

Tyler imagined Maddy grateful.

He forced himself to stop imagining and speak. "Well, I said I'd do it because I believe you. I'm glad you've abandoned your thesis."

He was very glad.

Thrilled.

He had no reason except common sense left to hate her now, and he'd proved to have a very short supply of that.

They lay side by side, his arm resting on her stomach.

It would have been romantic if dozens of strewn papers hadn't still been floating down on their heads, along with a cloud of choking dust. Add in boys screaming in the background who could burst in on them any second, and the fact that they had landed square on top of the place Melvin Melnik's rigid corpse had been a couple of days ago.

But except for all that, it would have been romantic.

His eyes focused on her lips. He pushed himself up on one elbow and leaned closer. A wafting sheet of paper drifted down and slipped between their faces.

LAB TEST RESULTS QUESTIONABLE AS TO FIELD MOUSE SPECIES.

"Maxie!" Tyler grabbed the paper. He pulled his arm away from Dr. Snow, barely noticing he had slid it behind her neck.

He heard her head thud onto the floor as he jumped to his feet, reading.

He regretted the thud, but this was important.

Further tests necessary.

Maxie might not be a field mouse? Tyler knew there were a lot of species of mice, but surely . . . He dropped to his knees just as Dr. Snow stood up.

"What are you doing?"

Tyler didn't even look up. "Here's a page, and here's one." He sorted and saved and discarded. "Get down here and help me find the rest of this report."

Something crashed in Maddy's building.

179

Tyler barely reacted. "This isn't on old paper. Well, not too old." Tyler held up the sheet of paper next to another one that had fallen from the same box. "Most of this is yellow and faded, but I can . . ."

He quit talking to read, and read, and read, and pray. "This is a disaster."

Only barely aware that Maddy had dropped to her knees and was picking up and discarding papers, setting a few on the floor where they knelt side by side, he finished reading the sheet in his hand.

Turning, he faced Maddy, who was still frantically hunting for something she couldn't possibly understand. "Maddy, you may have your thesis paper after all."

She sat back on her knees. "Why? I don't understand."

"We had Maxie genetically tested about four years ago when Wilkie was killed. It had to do with mouse fur found at the site of the murder."

Maddy's brows arched. "You genetically tested a mouse?"

"Well, not me, exactly. Liza didn't like Melnik." Didn't like? Try loathed, despised, ridiculed, sneered at . . . "So we weren't real involved with the town when this happened, but of course, everybody knew about it."

"Of course?"

"Sure, everybody knows everything about everyone in Melnik."

"They didn't know about my thesis paper."

"You'd been in town, what — a day — before they found out?"

"Point taken."

"So how come these papers, dated four years ago, are up here in this building, abandoned for decades? The building where we just found Melvin Melnik? How come nobody knows about this?"

Maddy, her eyes almost crossed in confusion, shrugged.

"Someone knew Maxie was a fake."

"He is for sure? He's not a . . . mouse? Because I saw him, Tyler. He's most definitely a mouse."

Tyler read the next paper. "No, it's not that he's not a mouse; it's that there's some question whether he's a field mouse."

"I'm lost. It matters if he grew up in a field as opposed to — in a hedge or a flower bed or a house?"

"No, no, no — where you grow up doesn't matter. Try to pay attention, for heaven's sake. This is important. Field mouse is a specific species of mouse. Maxie is the largest of his species. A world-record–sized Animalia; Chordate; Vertebrata; Mammalia; Rodentia; Sciurognathi; Cricetidae; Sigmondontinea; Peromyscus. In other words, a field mouse."

"How do you know that?" She shook her head in disbelief.

He could tell she was impressed. "You'll just have to be patient. I don't have time to help you memorize it now."

"What? I have no desire to memorize —"

"We studied it in school. We had to memorize it to pass fourth grade." Tyler had enough to do without explaining every little detail. "Anyway, Maxie is really big for that species."

"Does the state of Nebraska require that? I've heard of No Child Left Behind, but this seems ridiculous."

"No, the state doesn't require it. That would be stupid. Only Melnik requires it."

Maddy arched one of her beautiful dark brows at him. "Has anyone actually been left back for failing this test?"

Her brow almost diverted him, but not quite. This was too big for even slender, lovely, graceful eyebrows. "Of course not. Oh, they've been held back, but not for this. Everyone learns this. Don't you understand? Maxie's not all that big for some other species of mouse."

"Like what species?"

"I don't know. How am I supposed to know about species of mice? No reasonable person wastes their time memorizing a bunch of species of mouse."

"You knew Maxie's."

"He's special. But if he was, say . . . a grasshopper mouse?"

"A what?"

Tyler shrugged. "That and house mouse — mice — mouse — whatever — are the only species I know of. And he's too big to even possibly be a house mouse. So if he's some other species, then he's not special, and this whole town is built on a lie!" Tyler surged to his feet so quickly Maddy tumbled backward.

Tyler was too upset to try to save her. It probably would have ended in disaster anyway. Most of his dealings with Maddy did.

He ran into her building, followed the shrieking and shattering sounds, and found the boys in the dank, high-smelling basement, surrounded by mountains and mountains of boxes and cans and unidentifiable refuse.

"Boys, go down to the museum. You need to stay with Bonnie for a while." The boys, to a degree that was completely disloyal,

183

screamed with joy and raced up the stairs. Tyler turned to follow as he heard them run outside. But before he could move, Tyler spotted a case of antifreeze. It was notice-able because it was the only thing not an inch deep in dust. The case was torn open and one bottle and a cup sat on the floor beside the box. And right next to it, a manila envelope, clearly addressed to Dr. Madeline Stuart.

Maddy.

No way is she a murderer.

That was his male side talking. His inner lawyer had a different opinion. How much evidence needed to point to the woman?

No way is she this stupid to leave clue after clue, the man said.

She's a klutz; of course she'd leave clues everywhere, the lawyer replied.

But she just wouldn't do it. Impossible. The clumsy woman upstairs just doesn't have the makings of a murderer, and besides, she wouldn't kill to protect her research paper.

Look how easily she's given it up. The man had a kind heart.

After she'd been found out. What other choice did she have? The lawyer had a functioning brain.

And now she wanted to research Melnik about something else. She said she'd show

184

them her thesis, but who could force her to show them all her work? Who could be sure she wasn't writing a hit piece on Melnik for the college while writing a nice rah-rah piece on Melnik to appease the dim-witted natives, of which he was king?

Tyler took a moment to think about running for office. The mayor of Suckerville . . . he'd win in a landslide.

He looked back at the envelope. Her fingerprints were going to be all over it, of course. It had to be planted, but it wasn't his job to find clues and then cover them up for his client. That was a complete violation of the law, and he could be disbarred, even jailed for it.

But she was so pretty and sweet. Tyler's fingers itched to hide the evidence, grab Maddy, and run.

Maddy and his sons.

And Riley.

Running for your life when you were an adult with responsibilities was incredibly inconvenient.

Besides, Tyler knew he'd found the murder weapon right in Maddy's possession. If he covered that up to protect Maddy, he'd also be covering up a possible clue to the real killer. He had to tell Junior.

He sighed and then lured Maddy to the

car. Innocent little murderess that she was, she climbed right in. He drove her straight to jail.

Maybe Junior could just give her one of those electronic ankle bracelets. It would save everybody a lot of time if they could just keep track of her. Hopefully they wouldn't have to dart her like a rogue elephant and put a radio collar on her; although she was so aggravating, Tyler might volunteer for that job.

"Why are we at the jail, Tyler?" Maddy seemed calm.

"Well, the thing is" — Tyler turned to her, his arm stretched across the gap between their bucket seats — "you're under arrest."

12

"What now?" Maddy snarled as she opened her door.

The car hadn't stopped rolling yet.

Worrying she'd fall out and get herself run over, Tyler misjudged the curve and smacked his car into the Maxie statue with the police uniform that stood outside the station.

Bad day to be a mouse in Melnik.

Tyler got out quickly, thinking she might be making an escape attempt. Instead, she just walked, her shoulders slumped, sighing deeply, into the police station.

He had to hustle to keep up with her. Say the word *arrest* to Maddy, and anymore, she had a Pavlovian response.

Good girl. Well trained. Head straight for the cell or we'll whack you with a rolled-up newspaper.

Junior was doing a crossword puzzle at his desk. Tyler caught up to Maddy in time to see Junior lift his head and scowl. He must have been doing well on the puzzle.

"What now?"

"I found the murder weapon." Tyler entered the office.

Maddy turned to him. "In my basement?"

"Yes, sorry, but the antifreeze is sitting there, a cup beside the bottle, and an envelope with your name sitting beside it. Your fingerprints are going to be all over that."

"This is ridiculous!" Maddy threw her arms wide and smacked him in the chest.

"Well, you know we were looking for means, motive, and opportunity."

"I have none of those."

"You have all of those."

"I do not!"

"The motive is to silence Melvin after he discovered your report."

"That's a bunch of codswallop!" Maddy stepped forward.

Tyler braced himself to be accidentally knocked over. *Codswallop* was such a cool word. He loved her accent. "The opportunity is a little touchy, but your presence here in Melnik is close enough to the time of death."

"It is not!"

"And now we've got means. The poison is

there. You knew about it because your fingerprints are on something right beside it."

Maddy poked one finger at him and managed to jab him in the neck, vampire-like.

"Ouch!" It reminded Tyler that they hadn't followed up on all the town's newcomers.

"I'll tell you something you haven't considered, Mr. Master Sleuth."

"What's that?" Junior had come up beside them. Tyler noticed he'd stayed back far enough to be safe from the doctor's fingernails. Smart man.

"That report you're so upset about, bringing into question Maxie's true genetic makeup —"

"What?" Junior's curiosity overcame his cowardice, and he stepped closer.

"— was in Melvin's possession. And someone in town found out about it."

"No one's said a word."

"Report?" Junior came even nearer, but Tyler saw his cousin watching Maddy's flying hands like a hawk.

"You told me earlier everybody knows everything about each other. Therefore, it is absolutely reasonable to assume the word got out. Therefore, that gives a lot more people than me a motive to kill Melvin

Melnik. People who were actually in town. People who know what in the world anti- freeze is. What is antifreeze, by the way?"

She turned on Junior. Her hair whipped Tyler in the eye, and he considered wearing protective goggles around Dr. Snow from now on. Perhaps an entire line of protective gear. Flame-retardant suit. Hard hat. Steel- toed boots.

"Is the cell door open?"

"No." Junior produced the key from his pocket.

She snatched it. "I'm keeping the key this time. You chaps forget to let me out when I need a break. I might go to Jansson's for lunch, too."

Junior nodded and Maddy stormed into the jail.

The cell door slammed with a vicious metallic clank.

Tyler filled Junior in on what he'd found. Junior had a thousand questions, and they debated the possibilities for disaster.

The cell door gave its metallic clank, and a second later Maddy appeared. "I'm going to run back to my building and get some paperwork. I might as well be doing some- thing productive while I'm under arrest."

Junior shrugged and gestured toward the door to the street.

Tyler respected a hard worker. "Hang on a second and I'll give you a ride."

"I'll walk!" Maddy left, but Tyler heard her muttering. The only words he could make out were ". . . driving one block. Americans!"

She was so furious Tyler thought he saw storm clouds rumbling over her head.

She was so cute.

"We'd better go after her." Junior reached for the door.

"She won't try to escape." The fact that he had absolutely no concern about an escape attempt didn't mesh with arresting her for murder.

"I know, but we need to look at that basement without giving her time to mess around down there."

"And I was in such a hurry I left the lab result papers behind."

Junior gave a disgruntled look at his crossword puzzle; then he and Tyler went out, climbed in his car, and drove over to Maddy's building.

They got there just as Maddy stormed in her door.

Junior hoisted himself out of the car. Tyler didn't unlock his law office because he hadn't locked it. Why would he? There was no crime in Melnik.

As they entered the old opera house, someone crashed into him from behind. He looked back, expecting to find Maddy. Instead, he found — the whole town.

Tallulah in the lead, clutching Maxie's travel carrier to her chest. "It's a lie. A lie!"

She would have bowled Tyler over if he hadn't gotten out of her way. He rushed after her when something else clicked. Tallulah's name had been on those documents. They'd been sent to her. She had to know about them. And maybe she had the best motive of anyone to kill Melvin. She was committed to Maxie with a zeal that bordered on fanaticism. Even worship.

Tyler flinched. What would Dr. Snow White make of this mob? There were twenty people coming up the stairs behind him, all worried sick about Maxie.

When they reached the second floor, there stood Maddy. "I'm glad you've all come."

No one could hear her over the noisy crowd.

Tyler stepped to her side in case Tallulah attacked.

"I want to announce once again that I am not writing that paper about Maxie."

Everyone froze. Dead silence prevailed. They turned toward her like robots, all controlled by one huge joystick.

Even though, to his knowledge, no one but he had known about these strange genetic testing papers, somehow the whole town knew. And now not a one of them missed the quietly made announcement.

"I have reconsidered my paper, and of course, I can see how ridiculous my focus was on thinking you were obsessed with Maxie."

A crowd of one hundred people and growing, frantic to track down the news about the World's Largest Field Mouse, all exchanged guilty looks.

"I have already contacted my professor at the university in Omaha and asked if I could change my basic thesis question and deal with the general history and anthropology of your town, a classic example of many small American towns. Of course, his approval is required, but I expect to receive a favorable response soon. Also, even with his agreement, I'll understand if I've alienated all of you to the point you don't wish to speak to me."

Into the silence, Dora whispered loudly enough to wake bears, hibernating a thousand miles away in the Rocky Mountains, "What'd she say about being an archaeologist?"

"No, not archeologist. Anthropologist."

Maddy smiled hopefully at Dora. "I don't usually explain anthropology because it's a less well-known field of study, and I find people aren't interested in hearing about it."

Tallulah clutched Maxie. "You're not going to make a skeleton out of this mouse!"

Maddy shook her head. "But I believe in this case it would be worth my while to try to explain it to you. Anthropology is the field of holistic study with the intent of examining all aspects, both physical and mental, of humans, both living and dead. I received one doctorate earlier in my career in biological anthropology."

"Did she say they found dinosaur bones in Melnik?" This was Olga Jansson's father, deaf as a post, although no one could convince him of that. It was possible he couldn't hear them trying to convince him.

Maddy soldiered on. "My goal now is to earn my second thesis by studying the sociocultural disciplines. Anthropology, unlike the many other social science disciplines, is distinguished by its focus and emphasis on context, cross-cultural comparisons, and the importance it places on long-term, experiential immersion in the area of research, often known as participant observation."

The old man kept yelling. "I thought she was trying to tell people we were all nuts. Dinosaur bones could make us all rich."

Tyler saw Maddy lose the thread of her explanation. Just as well. He'd had seven years of college, and none of what she was saying made a lick of sense.

Unfortunately for them all, she gathered her thoughts and continued. "Naturally, an in-depth examination of all of these societal factors is integral to my anthropological dissertation."

"Tallulah, these papers have your name on them." Junior had obviously tuned Maddy out. Probably the wisest course of action. "What's going on? They're dated over four years ago from when Rosie Melnik smothered her no-good worthless husband while she had mouse hairs on her hands."

"Eek!"

Tyler didn't even turn around.

The *Bugle* was here.

Nick pressed through the crowd with Carrie in his arms. He grinned down at his wife. "Good thing your mom took Heather for the day."

Tyler felt a pang of jealousy. Not because he had feelings for Carrie, but because everybody knew how ridiculously happy the O'Connors were.

"I've also embraced the subdiscipline of applied anthropology." Maddy forged on. "My intention was to spend a short time with on-site analysis, because the general societal structure inherent in your hamlet has been well documented in case studies such as —"

Carrie snapped a picture of Junior shaking the papers at Tallulah, who hugged Maxie, while Maddy yammered in the background.

Tyler loved being home.

"All right! I'll tell you what I did!" Tallulah flung her arms wide, and since she was holding Maxie, she almost smacked Maddy in the face with the cage. Maddy fell backward, but Tyler snagged her like Derek Jeter going after an infield fly.

Between ducking the incoming mouse and Tallulah's sheer volume, Maddy shut up.

"When that lab report came back, it definitely had Maxie's hair tested as being that of a field mouse. But the lab said the specimen we'd sent had been compromised. There were field mouse hairs, as was to be expected when testing Maxie's DNA. But there were also house mouse and grasshopper mouse hairs in the sample we took off of Wilkie's face."

Carrie's scream peeled a layer off Tyler's

eardrums. Even Olga Jansson's father heard it.

"And there were a few stray hairs mixed in with the sample we took off Maxie's body, too. Now, of course, I realized immediately that the other hair came from that mouse-infested house Bea Evans let go to rack and ruin. So even though the lab tests brought into question Maxie's authenticity, I knew it was a bunch of hooey. So I tucked that part of the report away before I took the pertinent part to Junior."

"These are legal papers, Tallulah." Junior shook a handful of them in her face. "If we had taken that case to court, we'd have been in big trouble. By your hiding part of the report, a good lawyer could've canceled out the whole paper."

"But it didn't matter. It didn't go to court."

"Before this goes any further . . ." Maddy had more to say.

Tyler groaned aloud.

"Now you just hand Maxie over, and right this second." Junior stuck out his beefy hand. "We'll get these tests redone."

"Since you're all here, I just want to reiterate —"

The woman needed to drop the big words or no one would ever listen to her.

"— that I now see I was utterly wrong in my assessment of this community."

"Stay back! Maxie is a hero. You all want to destroy him! But I won't let you."

"I postulated the thesis that your interest in Maxie rose to the level of obsession, possibly even worship." Maddy smiled just as if she thought people knew or cared about what she was saying.

Poor deluded fairy princess.

"I can see now that you're all perfectly normal, rational, lovely people with a quaint mascot."

"I'm not gonna be the sheriff of a town with a fake giant mouse. That's just embarrassing."

Tyler flinched. Obsessed? What possible reason could Maddy have for suspecting that?

Tallulah hugged Maxie, and Tyler gave thanks for the cage, or by now Tallulah would have made mincemeat out of that mouse.

Tallulah backed away from Junior's outstretched hand.

"Don't do anything stupid, Tallulah. Nobody has to get hurt here today."

Tyler wondered where Tallulah thought she was going if she made a break for it. Mexico? Or perhaps she planned to take over a small Central American country and install Maxie as king and her as queen? Maybe she could buy an island and write a seriously disturbed Declaration of Independence.

Tyler started mentally writing a little thesis of his own.

"You'd've been guilty of . . . of . . ." Junior furrowed his eyebrows and looked at Tyler.

"Obstruction of justice, aiding and abetting in a felony, falsifying court documents, conspiracy to commit murder, an accessory after the fact, perjury, offering aid and comfort to the enemy . . ." Tyler stopped. He was pretty sure that last one had to do with treason. He didn't think Tallulah could be charged with that, at least not until she got started on her own country. There was definitely a thick layer of dust . . . not only in his office, but also on all his lawyer skills except contract law. Still, rusty or not, it felt good to use them, and no one seemed to notice the dust.

"Tallulah, give me that mouse. Now I know I seem like a hard-boiled cop —"

Tyler had to adjust his head on that one. Junior? Hard-boiled? It was possible the universe had a rule against those two words being in a sentence together.

Well, except Junior was shaped a lot like a

hard-boiled egg, so maybe — Tyler noticed Junior's comb-over was askew, as it so often was — nope, that detracted too much from the general ovalness. Junior was a big, affable, slow-moving, lasagna-loving teddy bear. No one could even imagine accusing him of being hard-boiled.

"But I am first and foremost an honest man. A Christian man, just as I know all of you are." He swung one pudgy, pointing finger at the town. "We aren't gonna base something this important to our town on something that ain't true. We're not gonna be a bunch of sneaking, lying, no-account, low-down weasels." Junior gave Maxie a sudden look as if he'd just thought of another species the mouse could be.

Tallulah inched backward, ready to flee.

Tyler refused to be any part of that car chase.

Whether or not she would have run was never known, thanks to the clumsy fairy princess in their midst. Maddy stepped aside to avoid the enormous approaching backside of Tallulah.

Honestly, Tyler decided, there oughta be a law requiring people as big as Tallulah to beep when they backed up.

When Maddy moved, disaster was inevitable.

Big surprise.

She stepped on one of her cuffed pant legs and fell. Tallulah retreated again and tripped over Maddy's prone body and went down in acres of fluttering fabric.

Maddy's grunt of pain made Tyler move before waffle marks appeared on her from the pressure of Tallulah's cellulite. Diamonds were created under less pressure.

Maxie somehow ended up on top.

The mouse had survival skills; no one could deny it. Really extraordinary in a dead animal. Tyler took the cage and handed Maxie to the side.

"Eek!"

"Oops, Carrie, sorry, wrong side." He switched hands as Tallulah tried to snatch the mouse back.

Junior took possession.

Tyler and three other willing — and brave — Melnikians helped a furious, shouting, struggling Tallulah to her feet. Tyler felt sorry for Maddy, but she seemed unhurt.

Flattened but unhurt.

And considering Tallulah was of the age to break a hip, it seemed best that Maddy had softened the older woman's fall.

Tyler helped Maddy up. Her hair had come out of its sloppy ponytail. There were pencils hanging here and there around her head — dreadlocks PhD style. She'd only been out of jail a few minutes, and she'd been pencil-free when they'd locked her up.

Maddy swung her dark hair. Tyler brushed her tousled tresses back so her face appeared. Her rosy cheeks had turned bright red, either from humiliation or from Tallulah's sheer weight.

Tyler began plucking pencils before she put somebody's eye out.

"So sorry." Her chin wobbled, and Tyler patted her on the back. He didn't want her to cry, but honest, if Carrie could scream and Tallulah could emote, why couldn't Maddy be the town crier?

He couldn't help grinning at her.

She scowled back. "I don't believe I have fully explained myself to the good people of this village." She turned away from him and faced the crowd, who didn't notice, because it was more interesting to watch Junior fend off Tallulah. Junior had one beefy arm wrapped around Maxie's cage and the other stuck straight out. Add a helmet and the man would look exactly like a life-sized, obese Heisman Trophy.

"Save it for a quiet moment," Tyler whispered. "You're never going to get anyone to listen." He went back to plucking pencils, but she didn't seem to notice. She'd said she was short of money. He tried to imagine her pencil budget. She could probably get by pretty well financially if she just quit needing a new case of pencils every day and a half.

Maddy frowned and whispered to Tyler, "I feel just dreadful. Everyone hates me and it's my own fault. I thought of most of those questions before I ever came to town. And for the first day or so, I thought I saw evidence to support my obsession theory."

Junior tucked and dodged. The former football hero and homecoming king ran behind Olga Jansson and her father, his very own offensive line. Tallulah came after him like she was the entire defense of the Nebraska Cornhuskers. She weighed just about as much.

"Now I can see that the thesis can't be denigrating." Maddy continued to whisper. "I had hoped to build on the eloquent work of the *Bugle.* I thought I could give real insight into the culture of one small hamlet in the United States of America. I had no intention of doing anything hurtful to this lovely town, even with my original paper. But I see now that the direction of my thesis was going to do just that. As usual, I've managed to alienate everyone. I belong in a lab somewhere, not even a lab with animals.

Just computers, waterproof computers, strapped down to the table so I can't knock them to the floor. I'm a complete failure." Her chin wobbled. Her eyes filled with tears. She looked back at the crowd. "I had hoped to make friends here." Her voice broke, and she pressed her fingers to her lips and fell silent.

As always, when someone whispered in Melnik, everybody paid rapt attention.

Tyler noticed Carrie's expression soften. She was a newswoman, so of course she was listening. He also saw Dora's curiosity bloom. The woman would need to forgive Maddy, if only to wring every drop of gossip out of her. Tallulah even paused from grappling Junior to give Maddy a calculating look — possibly realizing that a thesis paper about Maxie that made the mouse and the town sound good could be used in her master plan.

Tyler realized that Tallulah had a master plan and shuddered at the unavoidable chaos.

The pretty, klutzy, fairy-tale princess doctor had a chance.

Maddy was too lost in admitting all her faults to notice. And exactly when had Liza ever admitted she had any faults? Tyler removed the last pencil, and even with the whole town looking on, he might have stolen another kiss. His boys were even uniquely qualified to have Maddy in their lives. They had strong bones and didn't break easily. He'd up their milk consumption just as a precaution.

Junior shouldered past Tyler and stopped any potential kiss. Tyler returned his attention to the Maxie escapade.

"I'm going to take this mouse and have it tested." Junior held up Maxie's cage in one hand.

Tallulah's indrawn breath rose to near scream decibels.

"I'm going to lock these papers up tight so no one can steal them or alter them until the new tests arrive." Junior waved the documents with his other hand.

"I'm going to search the doc's building from top to bottom, and I'm not stopping until I've been everywhere just so I don't get any more surprises. I'm sick of surprises!" Junior reached the door and turned, glaring at the whole town.

Ben and Johnny raced out of Maddy's building, nearly knocking Junior down the flight of stairs. It was a good thing he caught himself, because at that moment Bonnie appeared at the top of the stairs and said, "I'm taking the boys swimming, Tyler."

Ben and Johnny raced up the stairs toward her then skidded to a halt, beamed, and ran back down.

Bonnie looked at Tyler and smiled. "Let me know when you're done here, and I'll give them back."

Joe was with her and nodded at Tyler, holding Bonnie's arm firmly as his very pregnant wife turned and followed the screaming boys, threading their way through the curiosity seekers.

Tyler marveled at his sister. She seemed oblivious to this disaster. Joe had definitely given her life perspective.

"No one else is allowed through this door. Except Tyler. You're helping me. Doc, you're still under arrest. Both of you get in here." Junior turned and stomped into Maddy's building.

Tyler realized he'd left his hand resting on Maddy's slender waist. He steered her in the direction Junior had disappeared.

"I really do most humbly beg your forgiveness." She looked over her shoulder at the crowd.

Tyler hustled her forward. She'd made some progress with her earlier apology. He was afraid she'd use her foot-in-mouth disease to lose the ground she'd gained.

He opened the door and gently but firmly

shoved her through, closing it behind them.
Junior was there to lock the town out.

He and Junior sighed with relief.

13

Maddy sighed with despair.

"I really should go back and try again to make them see how sorry I am." Maddy took a step toward the door. Tyler and Junior blocked it. She looked at Maxie, grinning at her from his cage, grimaced, and backed off. It wasn't that she was afraid of mice, just — ick.

Tyler held up both hands. "I think you softened them up a little." He looked like an elementary school crossing guard. And what did that make her?

She pulled up her pants and crossed her arms to keep them in place. She'd paid a fortune to have them tailored to this perfect fit. "Very well, let's search this building and find proof that I didn't do whatever it is I'm supposed to have done to whoever this man is.

"It really is outrageously rude of you to make me help convict myself of a crime I didn't commit. But I've got nothing else to do. You say this evidence that proves I'm the murderer is in the cellar? Well, let's go."

Tyler led the way.

Maddy was in the middle. "I can't help but feel you have me surrounded deliberately, as if I've attempted escape after escape in the past. The truth is really quite to the contrary."

Tyler glanced back at her. "We don't have you surrounded to prevent an escape attempt."

"Nope." Junior spoke from behind her, and when she turned to look at him, she missed a step and fell into Tyler, who nabbed her in midair like he was a goalie for the Manchester United soccer team.

He set her back on her feet. "We have you in the middle so we can catch you."

They reached the ground floor. "Well, that's quite gallant of you chaps, I'm sure. But as you can see, I've reached a ripe old age without killing myself."

"It defies belief, but what you say is true." Tyler pulled the door to the basement open. He looked at her, then past her toward the constable. Some sort of communication must have been contained in that look, or else Junior held up a flashcard behind her back, because without a word exchanged —

save a most unattractive grunt from Constable Cousin Junior — he passed them both, snapping on a pair of rubber gloves as he walked through the basement door.

"Maddy." Tyler stopped her by gently catching her arm. "I need to clear up about three things with you, considering I had you arrested a little bit ago. I hope you'll listen and give me a fair chance."

"A fair chance at what? Having me convicted and thrown into some American gulag?"

"Uh, that's the Soviet Union that had those, and since the Communist Bloc broke up, the gulags are supposed to be closed. I have my doubts — trust but verify, you know?"

Maddy didn't speak. She had no idea what he wanted, but she was sure it wasn't a debate about the current state of Russian politics.

"The thing is, I'm . . . I never should have . . ." He stepped closer.

She considered stepping back, but with her clumsiness, she might end up tumbling down the stairs to the cellar.

Tyler reached past her, intending to pull her close, she hoped. Then he shoved the door shut, and she knew that he, too, was worried about her possible descent, tail over teakettle.

Then he pulled her close. "I hope you'll give me a fair chance to tell you I care about you, Maddy." Before she could quite process his intentions, he kissed her. And then her processing ability short-circuited until she was really only capable of hanging on. His arms were the sure-footedest place she'd ever been.

He'd said three things. She couldn't wait for the other two.

She wasn't sure how long she'd been standing there, feeling utterly graceful for the first time in her life. But it wasn't long enough. Junior opened the door and hit her in the back of the head. She bumped her face into Tyler's. She was pretty sure she bopped him in the eye with her nose and possibly bit him. He ducked his head and brought his hand quickly to his lips.

Constable Junior looked tired and disgruntled, which was, for the most part, his usual expression. But perhaps this version was a bit more grim.

He held up a plastic Ziploc bag containing a manila envelope. Her address was written clearly on the front. He had a second bag containing a small paper cup. He must have brought the bags along, maybe tucked in his pocket, because she

211

hadn't noticed them before. "Dr. Stuart, you're —"

"I'm already under arrest."

"Oops, that's right. I forgot."

She put her hands behind her back.

Junior didn't cuff her. He insisted she needed her hands free to help search for more evidence to convict herself.

He actually seemed to have no real interest in her as a suspect. But the evidence was fairly condemning, she knew. They went downstairs together. The cellar was poorly lit, one bare bulb, a few small, dirty windows up high.

"It's mildewed in here. It smells terrible and it's filthy. I'm going to demand a reduction in rent."

"What are you paying now?"

Maddy told Tyler and he snickered.

"It is quite reasonable for anywhere else on earth, isn't it?"

"Yep."

She ignored his amusement and focused on getting herself un-arrested.

Nuisance, that.

"Since I have never even been in the cellar, I can't believe you'll find my fingerprints anywhere down here. They should at least be on the railing. You know I hang on for dear life at all times."

Junior had made her don gloves. She felt like a surgeon entering the operating room. She was very, very careful to keep them on so as not to leave a single print. "And that envelope, well, someone obviously brought it down here. Yes, it's mine, and my fingerprints will most assuredly be on it, but that doesn't prove a thing except whoever killed that man was trying to throw suspicion onto me."

"He believes you, Mad." Tyler was on his knees, checking the contents of cases of long-forgotten auto parts. "Just keep hunting through these boxes. Especially look for anything that doesn't fit, isn't as old or dirty. Like those documents we found about Maxie in the upstairs of my building."

Tyler stood suddenly. "Hey, Junior, someone's been down here. Look at these empty cans and bottles; they've been here for a few days."

Junior came and studied the trash heap. "It could be that Melvin was holed up in here, but we can't just assume that."

Maddy looked up. "Do you think he was down here when I unloaded my car last Saturday?"

Junior held up a copy of the *Bugle*. It had a prominent picture of Tyler on it. Headline:

Simpson Appointed County Attor-ney. "This is last week's paper. It came out on Wednesday. Melvin got sprung from jail a few days before that. I'd say he came straight here."

Tyler lifted an empty brown bottle. One of many. "And celebrated his freedom. He was in jail for over a year but never came to trial thanks to his lawyer's delaying tactics. He had plenty of time to plan what he'd do when he got out. If he sneaked in here and found those papers of Tallulah's, he might have started hatching a plan to use them to stir up trouble."

"He was spiteful enough." Junior bagged the *Bugle* and went back to sifting. "He thought he could get rich extorting money if his claim to Maxie held up."

"Yeah, but it wasn't going to hold up." Tyler bagged the beer bottle. "His case had nothing to support it. He had to know he was going to end up in prison and without a claim to Maxie. If he'd have quit plotting revenge long enough to just think, he'd have admitted that."

"Perhaps." Maddy looked in a box labeled Spark Plugs. Since she wouldn't know a spark plug from a hair plug, she had no idea what the little metal gadgets were. She couldn't imagine recognizing something important. "Perhaps he thought if his claim to Maxie became threatening enough, the people of this town would drop the charges against him for murdering . . ."

Maddy looked up. Her eyes found Tyler's, and her brain quit working.

"Gunderson. Sven Gunderson is who he killed. And maybe that's right." Junior paused to scratch his rotund stomach.

Maddy barely heard him speak. She took half a step toward Tyler and fell over the spark plug case that she'd just set down. Tyler caught her and kept her upright.

The constable cleared his throat loudly enough to be diagnosed with whooping cough, catching Maddy's attention. As she turned toward the constable, she noticed Tyler looking sheepish. He'd been staring right back.

"Keep your heads in the ball game, you two." Junior smirked. "So, Ty, it makes some sense, huh? Melvin figures he's got a shot at scaring Melnik into dropping the charges?"

Tyler shook his head. "You can't drop the charges on a murder once the count has been filed."

"Yeah, but you can plead it down; witnesses can refuse to testify. There's a lotta ways we could have helped him beat this if we thought it would save our town."

"May I interject something?" Maddy asked as politely as a schoolgirl.

Junior nodded.

"Unless I misunderstand this town greatly, which is possible," she added quickly before both Tyler and Junior could do it, "Melvin Melnik's plan to take Maxie away gives a lot of people besides me a motive for murder. I will, of course, add that I have no motive, except the very slim one you two have made up out of whole cloth. Whereas the villagers, many of whom are extremely worried about losing that chubby mouse, might see themselves as saving the town by killing the man. I believe we even mentioned your sister, Tyler. She seems sweet, but honestly, I'm sweet, too. Clumsy, stupid about people perhaps, but fairly mild mannered, not the murderess type at all, I daresay. If you don't suspect Bonnie, then you just have to stop this rubbish about suspecting me. I insist."

Junior stared at her a long time. "I really don't think you killed Melvin, Doc. It's this confounded evidence. I mean, I'm a lawman, and I can't keep finding proof and just ignoring it. It all points to you."

"Nonsense."

"It's not nonsense. I've arrested you and let you go and arrested you and —"

"I'm well aware of the arrests." Maddy

held up one hand to stop him. Why, she'd make a fine crossing guard herself, and what did that make Junior? "Although I suppose I've lost count. I might start some kind of spreadsheet on my computer to keep track."

Tyler snickered.

Maddy narrowed her eyes. "You know, the first arrest was because he had my necklace. Might I point out that if someone was going to frame me, they needed access to my possessions. How about him?" She jabbed her index finger at Tyler.

"Hey!" Tyler protested.

She smiled. "I'm just using you as an example. I don't want you arrested."

"Oh, okay." Tyler smiled in a way that reminded her that their kiss had been interrupted.

Maddy forgot what she was saying for a moment.

Junior cleared his throat and woke her up.

"Tyler could have moved my envelope downstairs. Didn't Melvin threaten your sister, Bonnie? Someone told me he burned a house down with her tied up inside. You two chaps have to admit that revenge is an excellent motive."

"You have the cutest accent."

Maddy scowled at Tyler and went on. "And now you find Melvin back in town, maybe hiding in your building; that's opportunity. You could have gotten into my building. That door to my flat wasn't locked the first time I came through. And you know more about automotive parts than I do, I'd imagine. So you'd be more likely to recognize poisonous liquids." She turned to Junior. "Means, motive, and opportunity, right? Half the town had better of all three of those than I did. Why aren't you arresting them? Because I'm the newcomer? Because 'Tyler wouldn't do a thing like that'? It's a bunch of codswallop and you know it."

Junior stared at her. He then looked at Tyler.

Tyler looked at her. "I didn't do it."

"I know."

"She's right." Tyler turned to Junior. "You really need to quit arresting her. You're just doing it now to be spiteful."

Junior shrugged.

"You could have the keys to my car and my checkbook, pathetic though my financial status is. That's almost the same as arresting me."

"Melnik — Like Being in Jail." Tyler spoke to the ceiling of the dingy cellar.

"What's that?" Junior pulled out his notebook.

"The town motto after Maxie's lab tests show him to be an undersized, anorexic kangaroo rat."

Junior nodded and went to jotting. Maddy had a wild urge to grab his notebook and see what in heaven's name was in there.

"The trouble is, I don't think you did it, Doc, but I don't think Tallulah, crazy as she is, did it either, and she's the craziest person in town."

"Except Clara," Tyler said.

The pie lady. Maddy fought down her gag reflex.

"That leaves Shayla, and, well, her alibi is pretty tight. I guess she could have snuck out in the night, driven over here, found Melvin."

Tyler nodded. "She could have been in contact with him. Meeting up with him wouldn't be that hard to arrange."

Junior tapped his pencil. "But I've got no physical evidence placing her at the scene of the crime. No fingerprints, no nothin'. Not even a snoopy Melnikian who saw headlights late at night. If it's Shayla, I haven't found a single thing to prove it. I'll take prints off that envelope and cup, but the way that was staged, I'm thinking the killer was mighty careful. I doubt we'll find anything. Or maybe we'll find your prints,

Doc, if he got the cup from your boxes."

Maddy did recognize the cup and her stomach twisted.

"So we've got exactly nothing, right?" Tyler's shoulders drooped.

Maddy wanted to perk him up. Perhaps she could offer to be arrested again. He'd found that cheering a time or two. Or maybe she could let his boys come and destroy more of her possessions.

Junior had his hands full of evidence bags. He reached one finger toward the circular ring on top of Maxie's cage but couldn't quite latch onto it. He bumped it and Maxie rolled, cage and all, onto the floor. "Ah, rats!"

"I don't think, considering the shaky status of Maxie's genetic makeup," Maddy advised, "you ought to risk saying 'rats' around the mouse."

"I'll get him, Junior."

"Okay." Junior flourished the Ziploc bags. "This will keep me busy awhile. Bring him along when you come."

"Sure."

"I think there's an attic in this place, too, but I want to get going on these evidence bags, then start the paperwork to have Maxie retested. I'm quitting here for today."

"We can poke around up there."

"Considering she's a suspect and you're her lawyer and I saw you kissing her earlier, that's probably not a good idea."

Maddy felt her cheeks heat up. She always blushed too easily with her ridiculous fair skin.

"I wouldn't tamper with evidence. You know that."

"Okay, have at it. We missed today's mail, so Maxie won't go out until tomorrow, anyway. Bring him along when you're done." Junior plodded up the stairs.

Leaving Maddy alone in the dark with Tyler. He took a step toward her, then another.

She didn't even think of stepping back. "Tyler, I want —"

Tyler walked straight past her and crouched in a dark corner of the cellar where Maxie's cage had landed. "There's something about this . . ." Tyler dropped to his knees. "It's almost like the mouse is pointing at something."

"A pointer rodent? Part mouse, part English setter? That genetic testing needs to be redone and redone fast."

Tyler gasped, fumbled in the corner for a few more seconds, then jumped to his feet. "Junior, wait up! I think I know why Melvin was killed." Tyler sprinted up the stairs without a backward glance.

Maddy studied the empty stairway then turned to look at the corner where Maxie still . . . pointed? Squares of clean floor. In this filthy, stinking basement, that was significant. She approached the spot where Tyler had knelt, mindful not to get too close and allow her clumsiness to erase any remaining evidence.

Something had obviously been here, and something had been removed, but what? And how could something not being here reveal a murderer? What had Tyler taken with him?

She waited a few seconds, thinking Tyler would come back down with Junior in tow. Surely the constable would want to see the . . . nothing . . . that Tyler had seen. They didn't return.

A floorboard creaked overhead and Maddy decided she'd just go along to them if they weren't coming to her.

She made her way upstairs and found both men gone. Technically she was still under arrest. She knew she had to go turn herself in but decided to shower and put on clean clothes before she went. Taking her time, primping a bit — God forgive her, she went back downstairs and noticed the sun had set. As she stepped out with her overnight bag in one hand — a precaution against another arrest — and Maxie in the other, she saw that Main Street was deserted.

She knew she'd been in America too long when she climbed into her Tercel to drive around the block.

A hard, cold piece of metal pressed into the small of her back.

She turned and caught a glimpse of a person crouching in her trundle seat. In the streetlights, she made out a dark hood pulled over someone's face, but forgot about that when her eyes focused on what was poking her.

A gun.

"Face forward and stay on this street. It'll take you straight out of town."

14

"It's drugs." Tyler burst into Junior's office.

Junior looked up from the padded mailer he was preparing for Maxie.

"What?"

"That basement — it stunk, you noticed."

"Sure, old basements smell bad."

"Not that bad. It was meth. I smelled it once before a long time ago. And . . ." Tyler produced the pieces of evidence that had tipped him off. A matchbook stripped of its cover, a striker plate from a matchbook, and an empty box of cold pills. "These things are used by meth-heads. I found them in the basement in the corner where Maxie rolled. They're what clued me in. Once I saw them, I recognized the smell."

"You think that pretty doctor is running a meth lab?"

Tyler snorted. "Pay attention, Junior. Melvin was running a meth lab. There isn't enough stuff there, though. He must have stored things down there, maybe smoked it, too, but I'll bet he's got a real lab somewhere. Probably with someone else, and that someone else killed him."

Junior opened an evidence bag. Tyler dropped his find in. Junior's usual good spirits had vanished. "I'm sending these to the lab for prints. I've had some special classes on recognizing meth addicts. It's a growing problem in rural areas, but I haven't caught anyone with it around here. That lowlife Melvin was bringing it into town."

With surprising knowledge, Junior explained what he'd learned in his training about meth. Then he phoned the county sheriff, who offered to call the crime scene techs in from Fremont. Junior phoned the state penitentiary and the state police. It was a maddeningly slow process, because it was after hours and no one with any clout was working late.

When Junior had finished, he turned back to the evidence bag. "They all agree it's meth. They're sending someone right out. Tonight."

"Setting up a meth lab is a talent Melvin might have picked up in prison. What did they say about his old cellmates who have been released? Especially ones with a history of drug dealing?"

"I asked for information like that when Melvin first turned up dead. I haven't heard back about anyone specific. The meth spin on this lit a fire under everyone — there's a big push to root meth labs out. The state police are coming in to help."

Tyler nodded. "Good. We can use all the help we can get. Now that we know what to look for, we might have more luck. Let's go search Maddy's basement some more."

Junior looked up. "Where is Maddy? Didn't she come with you?"

"She's right behind me."

"No, she's not. You've been here for nearly half an hour."

"Yeah, she is. I just got ahead because I was in a hurry to get this to you."

Junior looked past Tyler, and Tyler turned to see an empty street.

"Where is she?" Tyler asked. "It's a minute-and-a-half walk. Even if she fell over ten times, she'd be here by now."

"You left her? In a meth lab?"

"With a killer on the loose." Tyler whirled and ran.

Maddy surprised herself by not crashing the car straight into a ditch.

It was the kind of thing she'd do, especially

under pressure. And there wasn't much pressure greater than a gun stuck into your ribs.

The paved streets of Melnik ended, and with the streetlights gone, Maddy's headlights cut through the darkness ahead onto a gravel road. Slowing down on the slippery surface, Maddy tried to make her brain work. She was supposed to be smart. She should have jumped out of the car in town. She should have screamed for help.

"Where are you taking me?" Her voice shook, but it seemed wise to get him to talk. She might be able to identify him later, in the unlikely event she was alive.

"Just shut up and drive." The gun jabbed her until she knew she'd be bruised. The kidnapper was whispering. Maddy thought it was a man, but she wasn't positive.

Out the corner of her eye, Maddy saw whoever it was tug what must be a ski mask farther down his chin. The mask was a good sign. He must want to be driven to safety and released. Maddy wanted that, too. Desperately.

She decided not to try any heroics as she prayed silently.

Dear Lord, keep me safe. Tell me what to do.

"Turn at this next corner."

Not the voice Maddy wanted to hear.

She pressed on the brake too hard and the back end of the car fishtailed.

"Watch it!"

She let up on the brakes then slowed more cautiously. When she came to the intersection, she turned left.

"Not left, you idiot!" The gun jabbed again. "Stop!"

Maddy panicked and hit the brake hard. They were going slow enough that she ground to a halt without much sliding around. "I'm sorry. So sorry. You said turn, not which way."

The masked man — she was sure it was a man now; he'd forgotten to disguise his voice when he'd yelled — lifted his head and looked backward. "Okay, no one around. Back up and go the other way at the intersection."

Maddy looked in all directions, and the man was absolutely right. There was no one around anywhere. Her hand itched to grab the door handle and jump out of the car. Just run. He'd probably take the car and go. Her heart pounded. Her fingers flexed. Her thoughts scattered and scrambled like a trapped field mouse.

The gun jammed into her side until she thought he cracked a rib.

Coward that she was, she didn't have the nerve to fight back. Hating herself, she got turned in the direction he wanted.

"Why are you doing this?"

A laugh from the backseat made the hair on the back of her neck stand straight up. "Because if you run off and disappear, it's as good as a confession. They won't be looking for anyone else."

A confession? Disappear?

This sounded like a trip she wasn't coming home from. She had to get away. She couldn't trust to good luck that he just needed to get out of town and picked her for a ride, with plans to drop her off and steal her car once they were well away.

Still, she could almost feel the bullet from that jabbing gun tearing through her. She was clumsy. She didn't have the reflexes to open the door and get out before he pulled the trigger.

She drove for miles on gravel roads that twisted until she was completely lost. The gravel gave way to dirt. The flat land turned to rolling hills, then bluffs that loomed over her in the moonlight. The roads narrowed, and scrub trees closed in around her, slapping the car, grabbing at her antenna. Hardened ruts hit the car's belly on occasion. Her idea to get away from her assailant and run for civilization was a waste of time. The run part she could handle unless she tripped over her own feet, but finding civilization? Not a chance.

"Turn here."

Maddy slowed to a stop. Straight ahead was a grove of trees. "Which way, left or right?" The right turn was a lane with grass growing in the middle. She knew before he spoke that he'd want to go that way.

"Right." There were ruts deep enough to swallow her car whole. She eased around the ninety-degree angle, and with the bottom of her poor beleaguered Tercel scraping, she inched down the path.

The lane wound some more. Maddy's stomach twisted as sharply as the road.

She should have jumped out in town.

She should have risked it.

Now she was so far out that no one could ever hope to find her.

And no one could hear her scream.

"Where is she?" Tyler saw her car missing the second he and Junior reached Main Street.

Junior scowled. "She wouldn't run for it now. She's under arrest, sure, but she wasn't taking that seriously."

Junior pulled up beside Maddy's building

and Tyler jumped out. Before he could get Maddy's door open, Dora emerged from Jansson's halfway down the block.

"She's gone. Saw her drive away." Dora's voice carried with no trouble.

Tyler jogged toward Dora. "What are you doing in Jansson's after hours?"

"It's bridge night."

"Where's your car?"

"Olga gave me a ride."

"Where's Olga's car now?"

"She made a run for the Mini-Mart. She was out of decaf coffee, and she knows real coffee aggravates my bursitis."

"Did you talk to Maddy before she drove away? Ask her where she was going?"

Dora shook her head. "But I figured she was going to turn herself in. Or she was just tagging you. That girl's sweet on you, Tyler. And if it turns out she didn't kill Melvin, or she killed him for a decent reason, it's time you took a wife again. Bonnie can't raise those boys. She's starting on her own brood. Maybe if your hair wasn't so long and you picked up your feet when you walked instead of shuffling along, you could catch Maddy's interest."

Tyler fought down his irritation. Worrying about Maddy had to take precedence, and Dora usually knew everything, so he

231

couldn't afford to annoy her.

"She turned at the corner; that'd take her around the block to the police station."

Just then Olga Jansson emerged from the Mini-Mart a block to the west, dead in line with Dora's pointing finger. Tyler ran toward the heavily burdened woman. "Did you see Maddy? Dora saw her drive away."

"I was standing at the checkout counter. She went on past the turn that'd take her to the station. She went straight down the street." Olga pointed north.

There was Marlys Piperson, rocking on her porch swing, watching Jeffie pluck the neighbor's flowers. Tyler turned to Junior, who had finally hauled his girth out of the car. "Follow me in the car. I'm running down to talk to Marlys. Dora and Olga said Maddy went this way."

Tyler ran. Marlys pointed him on to the edge of town, near Bonnie's. Ben and Johnny were playing in Bonnie's yard, chasing fireflies. They remembered Maddy's car and pointed out of town on the north road.

Tyler reported to Junior, who had pulled up behind him. "Why would she leave town, and why that way?" Tyler thought of meth and the stupid things a person could do while on it.

Junior continued to tail Tyler down the street.

Mystified, Tyler stopped each person he saw to ask about the strange foreign car, and everyone he talked to had managed to spot it. Mike Sutton complained about the Japanese winning World War II by getting America hooked on their cars. Audra Tippins had been walking down her driveway to pick up her mail and complained about her no-account children who were supposed to run this errand for her and then complained that she'd waved and whoever was in the strange little car hadn't bothered to wave back.

A tractor running late proved to be Dave Blodgett. He'd noticed the headlights. "No cars out here at night, you know. I've got the last property for a couple of miles, so no one goes this way." He'd seen the car turn at the corner, stop, back up, then go the opposite direction of the first turn. He'd also seen, silhouetted by the yard light at his house, someone in the backseat of the car. "It was a kid, I'm sure. I just saw a head peek up between the bucket seats."

"A kid? Are you sure?" Tyler questioned people while Junior worked the radio to connect with the state police, gathering information about Melvin's cellmates and cross-referencing known associates with rented or purchased property around Melnik.

Dave shrugged. "Not really. I mean, it must be a kid, though. If it was a grown-up, why did he have his head below seat level, then pop up, then duck down again? No reason a person would do that."

Unless they were hiding.

"Thanks, Dave." Tyler thought quickly. Stopping at every farm was too slow. "Can you start calling everyone who lives up that road?"

"Sure, I'll have Ruthy get right on it."

"Just phone the ones near intersections. Let them know what we're looking for. We think she's . . ." Tyler tried to wrap his mind around a kidnapping in Melnik. He hardly believed it, and he didn't think Dave would ever take him seriously. But everybody knew Maddy had been arrested over and over for Melvin's murder. So how about . . .

"We think she's making a run for it. She's under arrest and now we can't find her. And . . ." Tyler came up with the killer, the guaranteed surefire way to get everyone involved. "She's stolen Maxie."

"Maxie? No!" Dave's eyes lit up with a *Law & Order* fervor. "I'll start calling. And I'll have whoever I call pass the word on down the road. This is the last intersection for miles, all the way to the highway. By the time you get there, maybe there'll be more information waiting for you."

"Thanks, Dave."

"Is she armed and dangerous?"

Dangerous only if she tripped and knocked you down a flight of stairs. "No, she'll come along quietly if we can catch up to her." Tyler didn't want anyone fantasizing about a Bonnie and Clyde–style end to this manhunt . . . uh . . . womanhunt . . . uh . . . mousehunt?

Tyler leapt into the car. "Someone's got her." He gave Junior the details while Junior hit the gas and fishtailed down the Blodgett driveway.

The nosy neighbor system for tracking someone worked better than the FBI's NCIC computer. At the next house an elderly housewife was standing alongside the road. She had seen the car cross the highway. She'd already phoned on up the road and had more directions. Junior didn't have to pull over for nearly five miles. By then someone else was at the end of his driveway, waiting and pointing and raving about mouse thieves.

They followed the directions. The roads headed into the most remote, deserted section of the county.

And then the houses stopped.

And so did they.

Junior sat at a three-way intersection. "Left or right. Which?"

Tyler's heart thudded. His palms were soaked in sweat.

Fear.

No one could help them.

A meth dealer — more often than not a user — was unpredictable, capable of violence, and this guy had killed before. "Where is he taking her? What's out this way?"

"It's not a coincidence this is a deserted stretch. Whoever's with her must have a lab out here. Nothing else out this far."

"But it's acres and acres of land." Trees and woods, untilled cornfields and pasture, lanes everywhere, twisting and intersecting. Too many to follow. "It's impossible. We'll never find her."

Tyler fell silent as he sat in the heavy darkness and prayed desperately for the Lord's leading. Coyotes howled; frogs and crickets chirped. Junior killed the motor and opened his window to let the night sounds in. Tyler followed suit.

All he heard was the high-pitched cry overhead of a circling winged predator.

■ ■ ■ ■

The woods closed in around her car, heavier, shadowed by brush growing up everywhere.

The Tercel had excellent high beams, and they illuminated the narrow and neglected lane until there were only the merest tracks and the grass grew all the way across. Maddy came around a hairpin curve and found a trailer right in the middle of the road. She pulled to a halt.

The decrepit mobile home sat directly on the ground, no foundation. The man reached past her, killed the motor, then took the key.

"Get out." He gestured with the gun. His movement aimed the weapon straight at her head.

It reminded her she had a head.

Use it. Think, think, think. God, help me to think.

What was the use of a massive IQ if you couldn't think of any way to save yourself in a pinch? She glanced at the seat beside her, only remotely aware that her eyes had gone that direction for no reason. And to Maddy, no reason meant a huge reason.

God had directed her.

To Maxie.

Maxie. Sitting on the seat. Snarling at the gunman. Obviously rooting for Maddy to get away. Maddy felt a spark of affection for the little creature.

Then Maddy remembered how some people, a phobic few, reacted to mice. Another idea out of the blue? Or out of the mouth of God.

She opened the door, her hand reaching low, toward Maxie. The man was watching Maddy's face, not her arm.

She grabbed the cage and lifted Maxie high and yelled, "Mouse!"

The man screamed and dove backward. His gun tumbled onto the seat where Maxie had just perched. Maddy kept Maxie, grabbed the gun, and, not wishing to even pretend to shoot anyone — though who knew what a woman might do in an emergency — ran for the woods.

Armed with Maxie, the gun, and — far and away most important — a God who gave people ideas when they needed them most, she tripped over the first branch she came to and fell on her face.

The gun went off.

The trailer exploded.

15

Tyler, leaning out his window, his eyes and ears peeled for even the most meager breath of a clue of where to go, jerked upright. "Did you hear that?"

"Sounded like a scream." Junior aimed his car for the field road on their right that twisted into the bluffs along Camy Creek. Deserted, the land was rocky and heavily wooded. A few open meadows provided pastureland, but they were even beyond farm ground out here.

"Yeah, a man's scream." Tyler glanced at Junior as Junior drove on the rutted lane into the woods. "Maybe Maddy tripped and knocked him over a cliff."

"Let's hope." Junior pushed the car faster. The rearview mirror on Tyler's door ripped off with a crunch of distressed metal.

Then they both heard a gunshot.

An explosion ripped through the night. The percussion hit Junior's car and nearly forced it off the trail.

"What happened?" Tyler didn't expect an answer.

"The ingredients for meth are highly explosive." Junior wrestled with the steering wheel but kept moving. The smell hit them. Fire. Sparks overhead drew their attention. Then they could see crackling flames in the thick woods.

Junior pushed the car faster over the ruts.

Tyler braced one hand against the car roof and with the other clung to his armrest. Window open, listening for a cry for help. Had Maddy been shot? Was she in the explosion? Was she even now dead, lost to him?

He'd blown it. Tears threatened, and he realized he was already more heartbroken at the thought of losing Maddy than he ever had been at losing Liza. He'd protected himself, and he'd lost the sweetest — a branch slapped his face as the road narrowed and the trees' gnarled fingers reached for him in the darkness. To get him to quit mourning and pay attention, maybe?

Something moved directly ahead. Junior slammed on his brakes. As dependable as sunrise, Maddy tripped and fell directly in front of the cruiser's headlights.

Tyler had a fight on his hands with a

mulberry tree, but he got his door open. Ducking under the branches to crawl on his hands and knees, he reached Maddy's side just as she was sitting up.

"Are you all right?" He knelt beside her and dragged her into his arms before she could answer.

"A man . . . a man with a gun . . ." She pointed up the trail. "Except . . . except no gun." Maddy held the weapon up and Tyler immediately relieved her of it and clicked on the safety.

Maddy and a gun.

The mind boggled at the damage potential.

"Let's get you into the car." Tyler looked up to see Junior. "She said there's a man up there. She took his gun, but —"

"Who knows if it's the only one he has. Weapons and meth go together." Junior reached for his sidearm; then his hand dropped away. He gave Tyler a sheepish look, as if expecting to be called a coward. "I'm not going one-on-one with a meth-head in the dark in this kind of cover."

"Me neither." Tyler helped Maddy to her feet. "Let's call the county sheriff and the state police while we get Maddy to safety. But let's do it fast. If he's seen us and he's not opening fire, then most likely he's clearing out."

Junior radioed for backup.

"There was a trailer house just sitting in the middle of nowhere. I think he was taking me there, until Maxie —"

Tyler pulled away from Maddy. "What's Maxie have to do with this?"

He followed the direction of Maddy's eyes to the little wire cage. She'd obviously dropped it when she fell. It lay on its side, with Maxie standing upright in the tipped cage looking fierce, guard dog-ish.

"A man kidnapped you and Maxie?" Tyler had thought the Maxie part of this had been invented solely by him. But to think this fiend had taken the town's beloved —

"Tyler, please don't say anything that makes it sound like Maxie's kidnapping was a more serious offense than mine. I'm too wrung out to watch my mouth."

Tyler grimaced as he realized, God forgive him, he was on the verge of saying . . .

"Maxie saved me." Maddy looked nervously up the road.

Tyler stared at her for too long then ran both his hands over her skull, wondering if she'd taken a blow to the head. "Maybe, just to be on the safe side, we could get you an MRI or something. You may need to have your head examined."

Junior came back from his radio call. "The county sheriff is on the way, and he's calling in a canine unit and sending fire trucks. We're supposed to wait for him back where we crossed the highway. We can call an ambulance as soon as we put some space between us and a meth-head with a gun."

Tyler slipped his arm around Maddy to keep her upright. There were less trees on the driver's side of the car, so Tyler supported Maddy as they followed Junior, who let them slide into the backseat. It felt like old times to be back here with her again. Tyler heard a twig snap, too close to the car — not at all in the direction of the fire. A chill of terror crawled up his spine. Whoever that was, he was out there watching, maybe armed.

"Let's get out of here, Junior. Now."

"Meth-head?"

Tyler caught Maddy up on what they'd found. "I went off and left you. I'm so sorry." Tyler realized he'd said "so sorry" with a British accent. She was rubbing off on him. And the thought of her rubbing off on him sent another chill up his spine. A really warm chill this time.

Junior reversed, his arm along the seat backs, looking over his shoulder while he inched his way out of the thicket in the dim red of his taillights. When they'd regained the bigger road, he switched on his radio to direct the county sheriff.

"You really think she needs an ambulance, Ty?"

Tyler gave her a once-over so thorough it really ought to have counted as a "twice-over." "About Maxie saving your life. Did he, at any point, have on a tiny red cape?"

Maddy swatted him on the arm. "No, the kidnapper was afraid of him. I remembered Carrie, and it's not only women who have a mouse phobia. I swung the cage at his head and yelled, "Mouse!" He screamed and dropped his gun. I grabbed the weapon, and Maxie and I ran. That's how Maxie saved me."

"Cancel the ambulance." Tyler exhaled with relief. "I guess she's okay."

He arched a brow at her, in case she'd overrule him.

"I'm fine. Shaken but not stirred."

Tyler was a little stirred.

"Then I tripped as I ran into the woods, fell, and the gun went off. It must have ignited a gas tank in the trailer, because the whole thing just exploded. It went up in a fireball from that one bullet."

Now Tyler was pretty sure he was both shaken and stirred. He pulled Maddy into his side, hugging her one-armed. She didn't scoot away.

Junior grilled her like a T-bone as he backed. Tyler felt the frustration as Maddy admitted she had no idea who had kidnapped her.

"He was in your car? He? A man?"

Tyler remembered Shayla was their prime suspect.

"Yes. I'm sure it was a man. He disguised his voice most of the time, but he shouted when I turned the wrong direction, and again when I swung Maxie at him." Maddy had Maxie on her lap, cradled like a baby — a baby in a wire cage — so — an abused baby.

Tyler shook his head and abandoned the analogy.

Junior drove, a thoughtful expression visible in the dash lights. "Someone must have seen him climb into your car. It's Melnik. On Main Street. On bridge night."

"But they'd never have just noticed and not said anything," Tyler pointed out. "It would have been all over town if anyone saw him climb into Maddy's backseat. I mean, c'mon, it's only a few feet from Jansson's."

Junior nodded. Maddy, too.

Tyler smiled as he realized she was getting the hang of small-town life.

"So this proves that whoever it was is new in town. Anyone from here would never have risked it." Tyler exchanged a satisfied look with Junior.

"Nobody in Melnik would ever think of climbing in there to hide. That lets Shayla off the hook."

"Unless Shayla's husband is helping her."

Junior tilted his head, considering it. "He might not know that the chances of not being spotted are one in a million."

"Melnik has a population of one thousand or so," Tyler calculated.

"One thousand one hundred and thirty-eight . . . Bonnie's baby will be thirty-nine. The town started to grow after the festival celebrating Maxie's golden anniversary four years ago. When Carrie wrote her first big article. Then that leveled off until Bonnie and Joe made the *Current Events* show with Gunderson's murder and Melvin's arrest. We got a population spurt. Those folks have been here long enough to know what's what. In the last year . . ." Junior did some calculations in his head. Tyler knew that because Junior's lips were moving and he occasionally moved his fingers, counting, maybe.

Junior muttered, "Carry the one, plus . . ."

"Sixty-six new people." Tyler didn't think

they had time to let Junior subtract four-digit numbers.

"Yep, half of them women, so . . ."

Tyler couldn't stop himself. "Thirty-three."

"Show-off." Junior scowled at him, steering as he backed. "So we've got thirty-three suspects. Time to start checking alibis on all of 'em. And it won't be that 'time of death' dance we had to do with Melvin. We know exactly when this guy kidnapped Maxie . . . uh . . . I mean Maddy."

Maddy scowled and crossed her arms. Junior kept busy winding along the dirt road until finally he rounded the corner onto the slightly bigger dirt road and they could run away even faster.

"He meant you, honey." Tyler hugged Maddy closer. "Have you ever noticed how much your name is like Maxie's? It was just a slip of the tongue. Thirty-three isn't many suspects. We should be able to eliminate most of them pretty quickly. Then we'll do a closer check on the rest. We may finally get to the bottom of this."

He'd called her honey. Maddy wanted to forget this whole murder and kidnapping business and try to get him to say it again. Then she remembered Maxie. "And don't forget musophobes. That man couldn't have faked that reaction."

"Musophobes?" Junior looked at her in the rearview mirror.

"People with an irrational fear of mice."

"We oughta put something about that in a wing of the new historical society museum." Tyler would put Bonnie on it right away, how musophobia saved Maxie . . . and Maddy. Carrie would probably help.

Junior met the county sheriff on the narrow road. They both pulled to the side and got out. When Junior's door opened, they heard the scream of fire trucks in the distance. The smell of spreading fire ruined the beauty of the night air, and all the forest creatures had fallen silent. Too busy running from the crackling flames to sing their night songs.

Junior bent back into the car to look over the seat at Tyler. "Take her back to town, Ty. The sheriff'll bring me."

"Can't we wait for my car and drive it back?" Maddy asked.

Tyler didn't bother to tell her the fire was spreading. She'd had a bad day; let her live with the illusion she was getting her car back. But Tyler knew the Tercel was toast. "Doubt he'd set up a meth lab anywhere without an escape hatch. He's probably taken your car and made a run for it. That may be why he picked you, anyway. Yours was the only car on Main Street. Maybe he climbed in planning to steal it, and then when you came out, he forced you to drive."

"So you think he kidnapped me by accident, just to steal my car? But he knew who I was. He said if I disappeared it would make me look guilty."

Tyler felt kind of sorry for her. It was almost like she wanted to be kidnapped for who she was, rather than just to steal her car.

"You think my car's gone for good?"

"We'd never get that lucky." Tyler patted her arm. "I'm sure we'll find it right away."

"It'll be a crime scene, so we won't be able to release it anyway," Junior reminded them. "If we find it, I'll get it back to town when the techs are done checking for prints. Then I'm going to want to talk to you, Doc. Don't leave town."

"I think you can rest assured that I won't. I don't have a car."

Junior left them to consult with the county sheriff.

Maddy, slumped in the cruiser's backseat, gasped and sat up straight. "I also don't have a purse, a checkbook, or my passport."

Tyler helped Maddy out of the car and into the front seat.

"It's much nicer up here." Maddy settled into the seat, touching the door handle. "And I can get out if I want." She smiled. "How delightful."

Tyler clicked her seat belt for her and wished that there was a seat belt he could click onto her for walking.

Maddy laid her head back against the seat and sighed. "Well, I've been kidnapped now. I guess that makes me truly an American. Perhaps I can become a citizen. With my visa gone, I may be stuck here."

"Not every American gets kidnapped, Maddy."

She arched a brow and remained silent.

Tyler drove down the ribbon of scenic two-lane highway while he wondered where-oh-where to put her to keep her safe. The whole "citizen" thing got him thinking. The easiest way to become one was also the easiest way to keep her safe. She could marry him. He'd be right on hand to guard her day.

And night.

Tyler's right tires fell off the edge of the pavement.

He jerked his car back on the road and his head back to the sunny side of sanity.

He pulled up to Maddy's building, and they both sat there staring at the darkened edifice. "You can't stay here."

"I know."

Tyler opened his mouth to say — well, no — he couldn't say that.

"Just take me to jail. I doubt your average drug dealer would go to a police station no matter how much they wanted me."

"That makes some sense."

"And I think, technically, I'm still under arrest. I was when I was kidnapped, and Junior must know I'm innocent, but still, he never formally dropped the charges."

Tyler looked at Maddy, even more disheveled than usual, which was saying something. She'd replaced the pencils he'd relieved her of earlier, and now she also had twigs and leaves in her hair. Her khaki slacks had torn knees and grass stains. Her pink cheeks were streaked with dirt . . . and maybe stained with tears. Tyler fought back the urge to pull her into his arms and keep her there forever.

She reached for Tyler's hand, and he let her hang on tight while he drove the block and a half to lock her up. He took her and Maxie inside. Maddy got a cell, although Tyler didn't shut the door. Maxie sat in his cage in the front office.

Tyler couldn't bring himself to abandon her, so he took Junior's keys and locked himself in the adjoining cell. He thought a locked door was best for propriety's sake.

It was hours before Junior showed up and woke him. Too tired to move, Tyler explained the situation, and Junior reported on the progress the state police were making on their end of the investigation. None. Then he agreed to let Tyler stay the night.

On a whim, Tyler fetched Maxie from the front office, oddly comforted by the presence of the disease-bearing vermin, and went back into the men's side of the jail. He lay down on the hard cot and watched Maddy sleep, relaxed, a mess, beautiful, through the bars. Soon the quiet night was broken by Junior snoring in the outer office.

As he fell asleep, Tyler made his decision. She needed him in a way Liza never had. He was going to propose.

Then it occurred to him that he'd never even told the boys he was thinking about going out on a date.

16

Maddy didn't need one second to orient herself when she woke up behind bars.

Really, it was business as usual. Hard to even get upset anymore.

Tyler was sleeping only a few yards away, also locked up. What had he done?

"Tyler?" She regretted opening her mouth the second the word was out. She should have let him sleep.

His eyes flickered open. His long lashes, each tipped with dark gold, framed brown eyes that met hers. Maddy noticed Maxie in his cage, hugged up against Tyler's chest like a steel-belted security blanket.

Junior entered the room, obviously showered and ready for the new day. "I had Hal come in about six thirty so I could go see my wife. She's getting sick of this case."

"Me, too." Maddy sat up and worked the kinks out of her neck and shoulders. "What did you find last night?"

Junior explained for a while, but it added up to nothing. Her car was gone but not burnt up, which gave her hope they'd retrieve it at some point. The trailer had been engulfed in flames and the techs couldn't get in until the twisted metal had cooled. They didn't expect to find much.

"Junior, can you stay with Maddy and guard her while I go home and change? I'll come back as fast as I can. But I don't want her alone."

"Sure, I'll run her home and stay on guard until you get back."

Tyler left. Junior drove her home.

Maddy didn't even think of protesting. She showered and donned clean clothes, her favorite khaki slacks and white blouse. She ran a brush through her hair and blew it dry. Normally she'd put it, still dripping wet, into a ponytail and get to work. Instead, she dashed on a bit of makeup, knowing it was Tyler who inspired her to fuss over her appearance. As she descended the stairs, she saw Tyler through her vast windows. Tyler, back already, and oddly enough, he still had Maxie. Perhaps it was too early to return the creature to its museum, but surely countless tourists were disappointed by the rodent's absence.

Her heart beat faster as she watched

Tyler's broad shoulders, and she nearly fell down her stairway.

Tyler escorted her to breakfast.

"Aren't you going to return Maxie?" she asked as they walked past the museum.

As they reached the diner, Tyler gave her an uncertain look. He reached for the doorknob. The bell jangled. "You know, I was so tired last night, I didn't even think to tell you —" He stopped and looked at her.

"Tell me what?"

"Well, it's only right that I warn you that —"

"Citizen's arrest!" Tallulah leapt from her booth. She skidded to a stop, her ruffled plumage quivering, her eyes locked on Maxie in Tyler's hand. Nearly catapulting herself, she snatched Maxie and left the diner in a huff.

"Tallulah, we've still got to get him analyzed," he yelled at her retreating back. He saw Junior waylay her, and the way Tallulah started flailing her arms and screeching, it was clear the lawman was retrieving the mouse to ship it off for further genetic testing.

Tyler faced the audience.

Maddy saw several folks muttering and glaring at her. "What did I do?"

"Tallulah's going to regret leaving soon and for the rest of her life," Tyler said, making his voice reach the whole diner, "because everybody else in here is going to get a firsthand version of the best story in Melnik history."

Maddy tried to see if Tyler was still asleep, just walking and talking, dreaming the whole thing. She'd done a bit or research on the effects of somnambulance and talking in your sleep.

"You're all going to hear the story of 'the day Maxie was mousenapped.' "

Maddy tried not to let it hurt her feelings that she barely rated a sentence in the story. Carrie came over from the *Bugle* office and seemed somewhat concerned over the part of the story where a gun was shoved into Maddy's side. But even she asked more Maxie questions than Maddy deemed rational. Not obsessed with a mouse, indeed! Why didn't they just put a crown on its tiny, furry head?

She glared at Tyler on occasion, looking for support. He'd just pat her hand and continue with his story. The questions poured over them.

Had Maxie been hurt?

How had he looked after the ordeal?

How close, exactly, had Junior come to

driving over him with the cruiser?

That question really bothered her. After all, she'd been holding Maxie when the mouse was almost driven over. No one seemed interested in her peril.

When Tyler made mention of the fact that Maxie had saved Maddy's life, the whole town flew into an impromptu celebration.

In with all this talk, Maddy found herself fed again. She never paid for it but checked to make sure someone did.

By jove, easy to find food in small-town America it was?

The thing Maddy didn't find was a simple answer to a simple question. Where was she supposed to sleep? Because she was terrified to be alone. Honestly, she'd been terrified from the first, but she wasn't willing to admit it.

Perhaps Junior would be obliging enough to arrest her again, although this kidnapping had to clear her of suspicion.

Pity, that.

Maybe she'd confess, just until the kidnapper — and mousenapper — was rounded up.

The constable came in and the whole round of chatter started up again. Maxie was in the mail. A definite meth lab, two sets of fingerprints found on things blown

257

out of the trailer. Mostly Melvin's, but they were running the others. Only a matter of time. The state police had taken control of the drug site and were right now searching Maddy's building thoroughly.

Perhaps the police would consider staying over if the search went late. They could sleep at her place.

She rose from her chair to go invite them. A few hardy officers would be the very thing to make her feel safe in her own home.

Junior caught her arm. "We've got to interview you. There's a detective with the state police who wants to sit in. He should be done at your building very soon. He's meeting us at my office. Let's go."

A collective groan almost drowned out Maddy's agreement. Carrie asked to come along.

Request denied.

Maddy headed back to jail. Her home away from home.

Although this time, surely, she'd end the interrogation on the right side of the bars.

By the time the state police detective was done interrogating her, with Tyler stalwartly at her side on lawyer duty, she was wrung out.

The police left and Junior produced a sheaf of paper. "I spent awhile at city hall and found utility records that really narrowed down our suspect list."

"To less than thirty-three?"

"Way less, because in that thirty-three are several children. We've had a lot of young families move in. I've got ten adult men who haven't been in town long. All of them could potentially be stupid enough to climb into Maddy's car on Main Street."

"Great. Want Maddy and me to split the list with you?"

"I've already made some phone calls. Three guys work overnights at the dog food plant in Gillespie. I confirmed that they were at work during the key hours. Two are on the Country Christian Church board and they had a meeting last night — it could be a cover, I suppose, but your average church board member isn't usually a meth dealer and a kidnapper. Olga Jansson's nephew's cousin's husband has moved to town. He was at Olga's house with plenty of company while his wife played bridge with Olga and her cronies."

"That leaves only four. Who are they?"

"The undertaker?" Maddy remembered him only too well.

"Adolph?" Tyler asked.

Junior made notes. "Yeah, I thought he

was a little shifty when I talked to him earlier."

"It's a cinch he doesn't have any friends to give him an alibi." Tyler leaned forward.

"And it turns out Luna Moonbeam has a husband. She's only been in town a few weeks." Junior consulted his notes. "He's been living in a . . ." Junior turned his notepad sideways, reading, his lips moving. "Well, looking closer don't do no good. He's been living in a sequoia tree in California."

"A tree?" Maddy scratched her head. "Like a squirrel?"

Junior frowned over his notes. "He was protesting loggers. Stayed up there for six months. He just got to Melnik a couple of weeks ago. I understand he's spent most of the last two weeks showering."

"That's a huge coincidence, with Melvin getting out of jail about the same time." Tyler narrowed his eyes.

Maddy thought he made a bang-up lawyer.

"Yeah, and it sounds like he's a nut. Do tree huggers go with meth, though?"

Tyler exchanged a glance with Maddy. They both shrugged.

"The tree actually makes the jail cell, and even my inflatable mattress, sound luxurious." Maddy found a notebook in her pocket, reached for her ear, and couldn't find a pencil. Tyler had relieved her of all of them last night, and she hadn't had time to restock. She wouldn't have looked in her hair anyway.

She plucked one out of the holder on Junior's desk and began writing. "Who else?"

"Wicksner, the new plumber."

"Dental Hygiene Boy?" Tyler tried to read Maddy's notes, but she scowled at him and shielded what she was writing with her left hand, as if he were trying to cheat on a test.

Junior nodded. "Is there anything else about the kidnapper you remember?"

"There is one thing."

Tyler and Junior leaned toward her.

"If this man is truly a certified musophobe —"

"What?" Junior didn't write. Obviously making note of that word was beyond him.

"A person with an irrational fear of rats and mice."

"Carrie? You think Carrie did this?" Junior shook his head.

"Of course not. But the point is, if the man was scared of mice, then he most certainly did not deliberately mousenap Maxie. He was definitely after me. I think someone ought to put the record straight."

"Everybody will know the real story by nightfall." Tyler patted her shoulder. "I just told them the dramatized version to keep them from attacking you."

"Forevermore, why would the citizens of this lovely hamlet want to attack me? They surely aren't still afraid I'm going to write a derogatory thesis paper."

"No, it's just that I told them you were on the run from the law."

Maddy looked over at Junior, who grinned at her, unrepentant.

Tyler went on. "I told them you stole Maxie."

"What?" Maddy surged to her feet, forgetting that her legs were still crossed. She fell toward the sharp metal edge of the constable's desk.

Tyler saved her and sat her back down. "It was a spur-of-the-moment idea. I thought they'd help us track you better if they knew Maxie was gone."

Maddy's eyes fell shut.

"Well, how'd you think we found you last night?"

"I don't know. I did wonder, but it's been quite a hectic time."

"But now I've told them all a much better story, and the word will have already spread

262

all over town that you were wrongly accused."

"For a while last night, it was like that old TV show, *The Fugitive*," Junior interjected. "We had quite a manhunt."

"Mousehunt." Maddy needed a nap.

"Are you done with her, Junior?" Tyler asked.

A significant look passed between the two men. It reminded Maddy of the look they'd exchanged yesterday before Junior went to the basement of her building and Tyler had kissed her.

Her heart rate picked up.

Junior heaved himself from the chair. "I'm going to Maddy's building to help with the search. Then I'm going to talk to Adolph and Jamie Bobby and Mr. Moonbeam. I'll be awhile."

Maddy sat there, not sure what her next move was.

It was time to make his move.

Tyler rose from his chair, and mindful of her balance, he took both of Maddy's hands and pulled her to her feet. "Maddy, we've only known each other for a few days, but —"

Junior swung the door back open, looked at their joined hands, and said, "Thought

I'd warn you."

Tyler immediately let go of her hands.

Ben and Johnny burst into the room, almost knocking Junior over.

"Aunt Bonnie's gonna have a baby!" Ben practically bounced off the walls. "Uncle Joe says we can't come because kids aren't allowed in the hospital, but that don't make no sense. We're not gonna hurt any of those sick people. We think sick people are icky."

"That *doesn't* make any sense, Ben." What had he been thinking? He'd almost proposed to Maddy without even letting the boys in on it.

"That's what I said. After all, they're gonna let the baby in the hospital. The baby's a kid."

"No, it makes perfect sense, Ben. Your grammar is —"

"Make up your mind, Dad. You say one minute it don't make no sense and the next it does. Which is it?"

"It's not about protecting the sick people, boys."

Again his sons quieted at the sound of Maddy's cultured voice and turned to her like they were flowers and she was the sun.

"It's not?" Johnny asked.

"Itsnot. Itsnot! It snot! It snot! It snot! Snot! Snot!" Ben chanted and danced to the joke. In the cramped quarters he smashed into Johnny, who stumbled into Maddy and toppled her over. She landed with a thud on Junior's desk. Tyler caught her before she did a somersault into Junior's desk chair.

He could do this. He could keep her alive. He set her on her feet.

She hung on to his arm tightly. Smart woman. Then she smiled at his sons. "The reason they don't want you there is to protect you."

The boys froze, obviously fascinated by the idea.

Tyler wasn't so sure. If the hospital personnel got a glimpse of his boys in action, protecting the sick people would definitely be a factor in any ejection. Still, he liked Maddy's spin.

"The people in the hospital are worried about us?" Johnny asked.

"Of course. And right now your aunt Bonnie —"

She said "aunt" like "ahhhnt" rather than with a hard — like the crawling bug. It was so fun listening to her talk. Tyler intended to do it for the rest of his life.

"— is very busy with the baby. Having babies is quite hectic, I'm told. And also a fairly slow process and quite boring for children your age. So she knows and the hospital knows you should be here with your father."

"I've gotta go catch the state police. I want them to check out Luna's husband." Junior exited, leaving Tyler alone with Maddy and the tornado twins.

"I think we should go to the antique store, then. I don't see why the constable should have all the fun."

"What reason could we give for going there?" Tyler had interrogated criminals and witnesses before, but felt those skills had been buried underneath all the contracts and wills of the past few years.

"She sells flowers, too. We can buy a bouquet for your sister Bonnie, and perhaps meet Mrs. Moonbeam's husband. The man who —" Maddy took a quick look at the boys.

Tyler realized they were hanging on every word that came out of her delicately accented mouth. "The man who talked to me last night mostly whispered, but I just realized I might be able to recognize his voice. I want to go listen to each of the town's newcomers and see if he sounds familiar. We'll be fine inside a business with large windows that open onto Main Street."

Tyler smiled. "Great idea." Then he said

to his boys, "You can come along and help pick out the flowers if you promise not to break anything. This lady's stuff is old, but it's expensive, and she'll probably make me pay in blood for anything you wreck."

And with the mention of blood, Maddy decided she'd stop in at the mortuary next. "We really should inquire as to how funeral plans are proceeding for Melvin."

Tyler opened the door and let the boys rush out. He laid his hand on the small of Maddy's back and whispered in her ear. "Another man, another voice, another big window?"

"Exactly. And I might need some plumbing repairs done, too." She smiled.

They were close, and the boys weren't paying them one speck of attention.

Tyler tasted her smile.

Then he propped her up when her knees gave out.

Having him around was brilliant.

Holding her upright, he pushed her on outside, grinning like a marauding . . . lawyer.

17

"I am Luna, your escort into the world of Moonbeams."

The woman stretched out a hand full of gaudy rings, and Maddy shook, careful not to impale herself. Behind the woman stood a living, breathing, six-foot Hostess Twinkie with a goatee.

Well, Twinkies could probably use a little fiber.

"Hello, we'd like to order some flowers for a new baby." Maddy smiled at the man.

His hairy, receding chin quivered with giggles. "A new baby, how wonderful."

He spread his . . . wings . . . that is, arms, but the wide bell sleeves of the floor-length Twinkie-yellow robe resembled wings, and his demeanor resembled something flighty.

In a tenor voice that would have been the envy of boy bands everywhere, he warbled, "Oh, Luna, my love, why, oh why have we never recreated ourselves? A child, what a wonder."

Not her kidnapper, not in any universe. Possibly full of cream filling, but no kidnapper.

Luna Moonbeam clinked her fingers together, and Maddy realized it wasn't just rings she wore. She had those finger cymbals on again, too.

"A child. Oh, Morpheum." Cling. "What a gift to the world." She swayed to the sitar music floating from a CD player behind the cash register. Her dress, a natural material of some kind — Maddy suspected hemp — swathed her undulating body in weedy splendor.

Luna whirled and embraced her snack cake of a husband. "Shall we, dearest?"

Maddy froze, afraid the decision might be made and acted upon right in their presence. She prepared to grab the boys and flee.

"About those flowers." Tyler's voice was a bit loud as he tried to direct their attention to capitalism rather than procreation. "Can we just order them now and have you deliver them to the hospital in Gillespie? Or should we stop back and pick them up?"

"Our flowers . . ." Cling. "Are growing in the backyard of our home." Cling. "We will give you the address and let you pick them

269

yourselves. Currently we have lilies, wild roses, and dandelions." Cling. "Pick whatever you wish."

"Uh . . ." Tyler fell silent and gave Maddy a wide-eyed look. "Okay . . . so what do we owe you?"

Cling.

"Our flowers are of nature, no more ours to own or sell than the water and air." Cling.

Maddy wondered if they paid their water bill. "It's time to go."

"Just set the beauty free in the cosmos." Cake Man released his wife with a bit of flair, twirling her like a New Age square dancer, an unlikely combination in whatever parallel universe they called home. "Take them as a gesture of love, as a gesture of being one with the circle of life. But give again to any you meet upon life's pathway." His wings flapped; his meager chin quivered.

Maddy didn't need to hear any more. The man's voice was absolutely not the one she'd heard before.

"That's very lovely." Maddy had no idea what it meant, but she wasn't going to pick their flowers anyway, so it hardly mattered.

"How do you make a living if you don't charge for your flowers?" Tyler didn't mention the antiques, but Maddy had noticed a

270

couple of price tags so high they curled her toes.

"Well, our trust fund smoothes out the ragged bumps of life, of course." Cling.

"Of course." Maddy smiled. She could use a trust fund about now.

"But we've had a breakthrough in our lifelong pursuit of bringing joy to all the living creatures of the planet."

That caught Tyler's attention, Maddy noted. Maybe he saw an investment opportunity. "How'd you manage that?"

"We've created an entire line of animal food that is completely in tune with nature." Luna did a swirl that brought her nearer Ravi Shankar or whoever was twanging away on the CD playing something completely out of tune with nature, to Maddy's way of thinking.

"Organic of course," said Morphine or Heroin or whatever his name was.

"It's an innovation, and we've truly considered the animals for the first time in the universe. We've made mouse-flavored cat food."

Maddy froze in her escape attempt. "Did you use real mice?" This was no assembly line Maddy would ever apply to work on.

Both Moonbeams nearly vibrated with horror. "We could never harm an animal in the making of our product."

"So . . ." Tyler seemed to be thinking it all through, very slowly. "You used . . . artificial . . . mouse flavoring?"

"Organic artificial mouse flavoring, naturally."

There seemed absolutely nothing natural about it, but Maddy didn't point that out. "And then . . . cat . . . flavored . . . dog food? And . . . and . . ." Maddy looked at Tyler. "I had a pet dung beetle as a child. Do you think . . ."

Tyler snagged her arm and started edging for the door. Well, he didn't have to drag her. She wasn't staying in here without him. These people obviously weren't dangerous, and yet Maddy had a powerful urge to run away screaming. "Well, we must be off. Thank you for your generous offer of flowers. We'll be . . . uh . . . sure to . . ."

"Release them" — Tyler filled Maddy's silence — "into the . . . uh . . . circle of life . . . or no, the . . . the . . . uh . . ."

"Cosmos?" Maddy supplied.

"Whatever." Tyler tugged her sideways just as she'd have backed into a ceramic pitcher with a price tag of seven hundred and fifty dollars. She was grateful that he kept a very firm hold.

She took a look back and saw his boys

272

make their escape onto the blessedly un-breakable pavement of Melnik's sidewalk.

"Thank you for your lovely gift of the . . . universe." Maddy stumbled over that, but Lunie and Morphie lit up like . . . like . . . well, moonbeams. So she must have gotten it right. "And good luck with the organic artificial mouse flavoring." That could work in Melnik. Who could say? Name it after Maxie, perhaps.

"Stop back" — Lunie sang the words. — "anytime." *Cling.*

Morphie flapped them good-bye.

They were innocent of everything but ut-ter weirdness and perhaps cream filling where their brains should be. No law against that . . . unfortunately. In solitary confine-ment Luna could cling to her heart's con-tent.

"Well." Tyler kept hold of her arm. Com-pletely unnecessary, but Maddy didn't complain. Earlier when he'd taken her hands, for a moment she thought he might be going to . . .

Ben ran out into the street in front of an oncoming car that stretched nearly the length of the entire block. The car stopped with a horrid squeal of brakes. The window rolled down.

Dora.

"You little whippersnapper. One of these days you'll break your neck —" Her tirade raged on.

Ben ran back to Tyler, who waved, ignoring the fact that his son had been nearly crushed under a car. "Thanks for being watchful, Dora."

Dora yelled a few insults, which Maddy took to mean, "You're welcome."

Tyler turned to Ben. "Stay on the sidewalk and don't run into anyone. There are a lot of old people. They break easily. You don't want to break someone, do you?"

Ben made that strange monkey noise Maddy had heard several times before as they walked to the mortician's office. Maddy saw Junior's car parked in front of Wicksner's Plumbing Shop just a few feet away. She really needed to listen to the man, no matter what questions the constable asked. They'd go there right after they visited the mortician.

They opened the door. An elaborate bell tolled out "Happy Days Are Here Again." A tune chosen because Dolph loved his work? Or a dreadfully misguided attempt to cheer those who'd had a death in the family?

The room had about a dozen coffins sitting around on the floor. There were none of those tidy little wheeled tables for them.

The caskets were right on the carpet. Perhaps inventory was expensive.

Dolph emerged from the back room, looking eager, hoping they'd lost a loved one, no doubt. "Can I help you?"

Maddy couldn't be sure if that was the right voice. She gave Tyler a quick jerk of one shoulder so he'd know they had to stay and listen a bit more.

He took the hint. "I've considered prepaying for my funeral."

Since the boys were currently yelling and punching each other while shutting the lid on themselves in the coffin in the front window, they weren't traumatized by their father's statement.

Dracula's eyes lit up. "Really? Prepaying?"

"Yes, and I'd just like to gather information. I'm not sure if I want to do it, but if you could give me some details, perhaps a price list?"

Maddy shuddered. Ghastly topic.

"Such a wise decision." The undertaker clapped his hands into one big fist — like nothing she'd ever seen a vampire do, so it diluted the similarities. "I've been considering putting ads in the *Bugle* reminding everyone in town that they could die at any time. Hope that'll drum up a little business."

The coffin lid slammed shut and Dolph gave the boys — or rather, the coffin, since the boys were inside and not available — an affectionate smile. "What little scamps. I loved to play in my father's coffin collection when I was a boy."

"Your father was a mortician, too?" Maddy wondered if the lid locked automatically. She really ought to check. There was an excellent chance there was no inside trip-lever in case a coffin dweller wanted to exit. Seriously, who would pay extra for that?

"No, he wasn't a mortician. What makes you think he was?"

"Because he had a coffin collection?" Maddy asked.

Tyler didn't allow time for Dolph's answer. "I tried to stop in last night, Mr. Torkel." And Ty also seemed content to let his boys play . . . dead?

"Please, call me Dolph."

Maddy could see the dollar signs in the man's eyes. She feared that Tyler was now Dolph's new best friend. Also his only friend.

"Well, fine, Dolph." Tyler smiled, his voice hearty and friendly and completely phony. "As I said, I tried to stop in last night right around dark. I didn't see you here, and you weren't at your house. Sorry I missed you."

Tyler left that statement hanging, with his eyes wide and generous, giving the man a chance to explain his absence . . . or alibi.

Dolph's sunny greed faded. "Well, I was . . . out for the evening."

"Oh, were you involved with the bridge club at Jansson's, then? I never thought of stopping by there."

"Uh . . . no. I was just . . . visiting . . . someone." Dolph's eyes shifted. His cheeks got pale. Maddy thought she caught a glimpse of a fang.

Maddy was no expert interrogator, but she didn't need to be one to discern that Lil' Adolph was lying his head off.

"Oh, really?" Tyler had that open, friendly tone still. "Who died?"

Maddy was swallowing at the exact second Tyler dropped that overly polite bomb of a question, and she choked. She bent forward, coughing, and Tyler slid his arm around her waist.

"No one died. I've got to get to work now; sorry I can't visit longer." The undertaker lifted a hand toward the door in a polite but unmistakable "get out" gesture.

"Are you okay?" Tyler leaned down until he caught Maddy's eye. Maddy, who suddenly found herself with the unexpected possession of mind-reading skills, knew Tyler wanted her to say, "No, I'm not okay."

Naturally, if she was choking, she might need a drink of water, a chair, lots of reasons to stay a minute or two longer.

"I'm . . . I'm not —" Maddy tossed in a new fit of coughing. She'd taken a few drama courses in high school before her teacher politely told her they couldn't afford the scenery repair costs.

Tyler patted her on the back. "Could she sit down, maybe?"

"Something just went down the wrong way." Her fake choking escalated until she really choked. Acting had never been her gift.

Dolph, lying liar, un-dead bloodsucker or not, couldn't very well let her choke to death. The town might see it as him trying to drum up business. Bad show all around, that.

"Sure, uh . . ." He looked around somewhat desperately. Other than the coffins and Dolph's desk, the room was full and there were no chairs. Maddy wondered if he'd offer them a seat on one of his cut-rate pine boxes.

"Come on into the back room." He acted as though they'd asked him to make an organ donation — immediately and without anesthetic.

Tyler called over his shoulder. "When you're done in the coffin, boys, come on into the back."

Dolph flinched.

Maddy elbowed Tyler then threw in another gut-wrenching cough for good measure.

As they passed through fabric curtains that separated the front of the store from the back, Maddy wondered if it was so smart to sequester themselves with a possible murderer.

18

"Well?" Tyler fetched the boys out of the coffin while he watched Maddy for possible clues that she'd recognized Torkel's voice.

It had taken some doing to find his sons. They'd moved on to a different casket. On the fourth try, Johnny did a jack-in-the-box imitation when Tyler opened the lid.

Pop goes the weasel, indeed.

Ben was in sarcophagus number eight. Lifting his son out, Tyler noticed footprints in the shirred silk lining and hoped the coffin would still sell.

No one, but no one, wanted a used casket.

When they reached the sidewalk, Maddy said, "I just can't tell."

She looked helpless, her pretty blue eyes round and confused. She was thinking so hard, her feet were even more "both left-ish" than usual, so Tyler held her arm for every step.

"But it's possible it's him?"

"Yes, it's possible, but I could never swear to it in court. Wouldn't that be necessary if I identified him?"

Tyler nodded. Unless they could scare a confession out of him. "He was definitely hiding something. I think he just went to number one on our suspect list. Let's try the plumber next. Junior should have been in and out. Uh . . . I think I need a new sink in the bathroom at my law office."

"Let's hope it's more fun than planning your funeral. Really, Tyler, did you have to go with the cheapest coffin he had?"

One of the boys disappeared in the vacant lot. A green space created when Dora managed, with one badly aimed car, to collapse the former home of the Melnik Historical Society Museum.

"Well, it made me mad when he called it the Welfare Casket. I mean, talk about language designed to make a grieving family pay more."

"Yes, but still, he's right; we might as well wrap you in an old blanket and just toss you in a shallow grave in the woods as use that one. A little dignity, please."

"I didn't sign anything. I have no intention of planning my funeral at my age."

"What was that he said?"

Tyler snorted. "He said, 'If you want to be

buried like Rover, I can bury you like Rover.' The smug jerk."

"Well, I'm glad you've decided to delay your decision, because you proved to be dreadful at it."

Tyler snickered.

"But his hopes were so high. Poor man."

"He'll get over it." Ben reappeared, and Tyler yelled ahead, "Boys, go on into the museum. It's Carrie's afternoon off, and she's running things while Bonnie has her baby."

"Carrie O'Connor?" Maddy gaped.

"Sure, why not?"

"Will Maxie be safe? She hates him. I mean, she'd have to touch him to throw him away, but . . ."

"That'll save him." Tyler smiled. She was already starting to think like a Melnikian. "But thanks for worrying about him. We mailed him off to be genetically tested, re-member?"

Maddy snorted. The boys vanished into the museum. Carrie came outside and waved. "I've got 'em, Ty, but you and Maddy owe me an interview about this case."

"It's a deal. Have you heard anything more about Bonnie?" Tyler waved back.

"Nope, but everybody knows it'll be slow.

282

Joe insisted on taking her in at the first twinge. We probably won't hear anything for hours."

"Thanks. I'll drive over later." Tyler took Maddy's arm and turned her around to go back to Jamie Bobby Wicksner's plumbing store.

There was no one on the sidewalk, but several cars sat in front of Jansson's, including Dora's boat. It was a very old Chrysler New Yorker, but Dora had come forward nearly two decades when she'd replaced the car that now lived under the vacant lot. It had been easier to bury it and plant a rock garden than drag it out after the museum disaster.

They passed the bright blue monster. Dora must buy cars by the foot.

They passed Jansson's and reached Wicksner's Plumbing Shop. The letters were smeared stencils on the front-door window.

Tyler twisted the knob and set a bell jingling as they entered a disaster.

This building held some wonderful childhood memories for Tyler. This was the old pharmacy. It reminded him of ice cream. The former owners had abandoned the elaborate soda fountain business long before Tyler's time, but they'd had ice cream cones in the summer, and his mom had taken him here after swimming and talked about egg creams and malted chocolate, and how she and Tyler's father had come here when they were dating. The marble counter still lined one wall with a row of low black vinyl stools that would spin when a kid sat down and pushed. But the counter was now buried in an unidentifiable muddle of pipes, tools, spare plumbing parts, and oily rags.

It was a disaster so bad, so filthy, Tyler began to long for the pleasant atmosphere of coffins. "Hello, is anybody here?"

No one was out front and no one came from the back to greet them. The floor was piled with boxes, torn open, overflowing. Obviously stuff that had been moved in here by Jamie Bobby. The building had been abandoned for years, but Tyler knew the Morgans, who had run the place for two generations. They'd have never left this refuse behind. It would have offended their sense of decency.

"Mr. Wicksner?" Only silence. "I need a plumber."

A thin trail twisted through the stacks of junk. An entire air conditioner unit sat near the front door. There were boxes piled on top of it and odds and ends of metal and wire on top of the boxes. A rusting furnace lay on its side between a dozen propane cans marked REFRIGERANT. Tyler saw a rusted-out water heater behind the furnace.

Tools of all kinds were tossed into the mess. A collection of huge pipe wrenches, coated in grease, were scattered among open cases of pipes and wires and unidentifiable metal gizmos. Junk, stacked chest high, everywhere. Maybe the mess made sense to Jamie Bobby, but Tyler's orderly soul couldn't imagine functioning in this chaos.

"No one is here, I guess. Let's see if he's out back." He caught Maddy's arm firmly and pulled her along behind him, taking each step carefully. A fall in here could mean death, or at the very least, he could lose her in the catastrophic clutter and have a real hard time finding her again. He carefully skirted a fifty-gallon iron oil drum with its top cut off so jaggedly that it could become a lethal weapon. He made a mental note to check when he'd last had a tetanus shot.

He inched along the narrow opening, hoping whatever earthquake caused this mess didn't hit again.

"How long has he been in this building?" Maddy whispered in Tyler's ear.

Her breath on his ear made him forget the mess, and Jamie Bobby and Melvin

Melnik and the Welfare Casket.

And his own name.

He turned to give her his full attention. She was too close and her eyes were too blue and his death grip on her arm relaxed at the same time he pulled her closer.

"You know, Maddy, earlier I wanted to . . ." He shook his head. He was doing it again. He had to talk to the boys first. "Uh . . . not long."

" 'Earlier you wanted to . . . uh, not long'? Whatever does that mean?"

"It means Wicksner hasn't been in the building long. Just a few weeks, I think." Tyler needed to have something done to keep his mind on the murder — a taser gun applied to his backside on occasion, maybe. It really shouldn't have been so hard, but surprisingly, thanks to Maddy, it was.

"How could anyone make this much mess in only a matter of weeks?"

"He must be some kind of obsessive-compulsive packrat. A complete slob who —"

"Tyler." Maddy interrupted him and tugged on his arm, but he knew better than to let her roam around free.

"— never cleans, never throws a thing away, kids himself that this mountain of garbage has a lot of valuable stuff in it." Tyler was on a roll, indignant at such disorder in the orderly town of Melnik. "I'll bet he trashes any room he enters."

"Tyler, maybe you should —"

But Tyler thought about the Morgans and the pride they'd taken in their tidy drugstore. "He ought to be horsewhipped. This building was beautiful. It's a crime what he's doing to this —"

"A crime, Mr. Big Shot Lawyer?" A deep voice sounded like it was only a couple of feet behind him.

Tyler flinched. "Oops."

Maddy gave him a sympathetic grimace, and he knew then that she'd been trying to warn him.

"A crime's what an honest man has to pay for a lawyer in this country."

Tyler turned to face the perfectly innocent slob he'd just insulted. He let go of Maddy for a minute while he turned, but he knew what was important and grabbed hold again, to shield her from Wicksner's temper and to keep her from falling.

The man stormed forward, his teeth — tooth — bared right in Tyler's face. Wicksner had a week's growth of beard, hair as greasy as the rags littering the shop, and blue denim overalls over a red plaid flannel shirt. Both articles of clothing were more black than any other color.

"I'm sorry, Mr. Wicksner."

"Keep it! I don't want your apology. Get out of my shop." Wicksner was about four inches shorter than Tyler's six feet, and he was whipcord lean, not an ounce of fat on him.

Tyler remembered the plan. Keep him talking. Just because Tyler was now trying to speak around his size twelve wingtips that he'd so neatly inserted into his own mouth didn't mean the plan could be abandoned. Of course, the man had already talked.

With a glance at Maddy, Tyler could tell she was still listening, which must mean she needed to hear more. Tyler wanted to run, but this detective business called for a backbone. "I am sorry. I had no right to speak about you that way. I need a plumber."

"I won't do business with you. I want you out of here." The man swung an arm, long enough to drag his knuckles and impress a female gorilla, in a wide arc.

Tyler braced himself as he looked at the furious man. And the bad part was, Tyler deserved this. He'd been gossiping like an old woman.

Then he mentally apologized to old women who had no monopoly on gossip.

"No, I won't leave. I've made you angry, and I deserve it, so I'm staying. Have your say, Mr. Wicksner. I'll take it." Tyler had stuck his foot in his mouth a few other times in his life. Who hadn't? But he liked to think he was man enough to stand up and take any criticism he had coming. But Jamie Bobby Wicksner was a hard man to stand up to. Partly because he was so violently angry, and partly because he smelled bad.

"My name is Tyler Simpson. I spent a lot of time in this store as a kid, and I came in here remembering a tidy little drugstore. But this is your place and you've got a right to keep it however suits you. We want new people in Melnik and new businesses on Main Street, and I don't want my actions to hurt the town. I was rude. I was out of line, and I apologize."

"Nothing could hurt this dump of a town any worse'n it's already hurt. And I'll starve before I take one penny of your business. Now get out!"

Wicksner took a menacing step forward. Tyler could take him . . . maybe. But a brawl wasn't going to solve anything. One false step and Tyler would impale himself on a broken water heater anyway, and drag poor Maddy down with him, so retreat was in order.

"All right, we're leaving." Tyler switched his grip on Maddy's wrist from his left hand to his right, hoping he steered in reverse better with his dominant hand. He backed away from Wicksner — the place was almost too narrow to turn around in, anyway. The bell above the door jangled when Maddy pulled it open. The two of them stepped out and Jamie Bobby slammed the door in Tyler's face.

Breathing slowly to steady himself, Tyler decided it was safe to look away from the glowering plumber who now glared at them through his glass front door, guarding his domain like a toothless pit bull.

Tyler pulled Maddy down the street, past Jansson's, past Moonbeam's, even past the Melnik Historical Society Museum. When he got to his building, he dragged Maddy inside then turned to watch his flank for sneak attacks.

When he decided the coast was clear, he turned to Maddy. "Well, did you recognize his voice?"

Maddy shook her head. "No more than I recognized Mr. Torkel's. I just can't be sure, Tyler. He whispered most of the time. The one time he shouted, well, it was shouting, loud, no noticeable accent." Her shoulders slumped. "I just can't be sure."

19

"We'll get the rest of the list of newcomers from Junior and figure out a way to talk to all of them." Tyler realized that what he'd wished for all day had finally happened. He'd gotten Dr. Snow alone. His hands seemed to move involuntarily to take hers.

She looked from his hands to his eyes, no doubt remembering he'd done this before.

"Maddy, I know we've met under strange, difficult circumstances."

"I whacked you in the face with a door; then we found a dead body."

"And I haven't always been as nice as possible."

"You personally arrested me once, and assisted any number of times."

"But I like to think we've gotten to know each other, and I care —"

"What's that?" She cut him off, staring at the floor.

Tyler looked down. He was standing on

an envelope. A letter addressed to Dr. Madeline Stuart. In his law office?

"Have you told the post office your address yet?"

Maddy shook her head. "I've been in jail far too much to make such mundane arrangements. But still, everybody knows I'm in town. Why wouldn't the mailman drop it at my building?"

Tyler shrugged. "Maybe he meant to and just got mixed up. Maybe he knows I'm your attorney and figured I'd get it to you."

"I'm not sure that's precisely legal. Doesn't America have postal inspectors?" Maddy dropped his hands and bent to pick up the letter. Tyler wisely stayed back to keep from banging heads. She straightened and looked at the return address.

"It's from my professor in Omaha." Her eyes brightened. "I expected him to phone or e-mail, but of course my phone doesn't work, and I'm not online."

"Your grades for the class you just finished?"

"No, this will be permission to change my thesis topic. Once I have this, I'll know my project can proceed." She ripped the envelope open eagerly, smiling.

Tyler loved her enthusiasm. She might be a bit clumsy and have a knack for getting arrested, but she was definitely a smart little thing.

Her eyes ran back and forth as she read the letter, and the smile melted from her lips. "It's not approved."

"What?" Tyler reached for the letter without thinking to ask. He scanned the page. "He says it's been done before, too much. You can return to your original thesis or —" The paper dropped to the floor as he looked at her.

"Or drop the program, which means my student visa expires immediately and I have to go home."

Tyler shook his head. "No, you don't have to go home. Not if you marry me."

Maddy's forehead furrowed. "What?"

Tyler took her hands again. "Marry me, Maddy."

He hadn't told his sons yet.

Dear God, I can't do this without talking to them, finding out if they can accept her.

He should have had all summer to decide, months, but now the time was up. And he should have asked the boys. What was he thinking?

He tried to control the internal flinch, but he was looking right at her and she must have sensed it, because she shook her hands free.

"Thank you, Tyler, but that hardly seems like a good reason to marry."

"No, that's not how I meant it. I lo . . . lo . . ." Tyler stumbled on the word *love*. He knew that's what he should say. But he just couldn't. He cared about her. But he needed more time before he'd love her.

Oh, he'd marry her. He was sure she wasn't as controlling and unkind as Liza. And look how long he'd stuck that out.

Being married to Maddy would be a lot more fun than being married to Liza; it'd be great. They'd make it. He'd eventually love her. But knowing that in his head wasn't the same as trusting it in his heart. So they'd get married for sensible reasons and let emotions come later.

"Maddy, you know I care about you." He grabbed both her hands again, holding on tight this time.

"Do I?"

"Well, yes. I've kissed you a couple of times. We have fun. You're so beautiful; how could I not care about you?"

Maddy held his gaze, and he was struck again by how smart she was. He felt as if she was boring into his brain, reading his thoughts, weighing all the pros and cons like he'd asked her to balance an equation instead of marry him.

And guilt made him cranky. "It's not that hard a question, Maddy. You either want to marry me or not."

Maddy looked down at their joined hands a long time. "I think the answer is 'not,' Tyler. Thank you for trying to rescue me from deportation, but I'm not exactly being sent back to my death in a third-world country. Britain is a lovely place. I'll be fine."

She pulled away. "I'd best go clear it with Junior before I leave the country. I'm not sure if he's got the paperwork done to drop the charges on me for my last arrest. And he may need me as a witness about the kidnapping."

Tyler stood like a hundred and eighty pounds of dumb, blocking the door. She tried to step past him, but he wouldn't let her by. It reminded him of when he was married and he didn't make a move without Liza telling him to. There came a point when he would've needed his wife to tell him to step out of the way of an oncoming semi.

Maddy smiled, but it was a smile that made Tyler want to cry. Then she turned and walked up his steps. Frozen, wanting to go after her, knowing he needed to talk to the boys, he didn't move. He needed time; he needed to write a persuasive closing argument; he needed to grow a spine and relearn how to think for himself. He needed all of that before he got married again.

So he let her go.

He heard the door to her building open and close. Then he went to his stupid desk in his stupid law office and sat down in his stupid chair and wondered how he'd ever gotten so stupid.

Then determination settled down right on his stupid shoulders and he reached for the phone to call Carrie and get his boys. He wasn't letting Maddy go, but he'd do things the right way.

First, he'd talk to his boys.

Maddy sank onto her inflatable bed.

She could feel her hand, still warm from Tyler's touch. He'd proposed. Tears burned her eyes. It was the first proposal she'd ever had.

It wasn't lost on her that they'd never been on a date.

So, since no one else had ever asked her on a date — not counting an ill-fated school dance with her cousin Gerard — she'd had a proposal before she'd had a first date. For some reason that broke her heart.

What it amounted to was, he'd had a gallant white-knight reflex when he realized she was going to have to give up on her schooling. He'd rescued her. But fundamentally what it meant was, he didn't know her well enough to reject her. And she wasn't going to grab his proposal and say yes, then let him find out the bad news — that he was married to a colossal twit — at leisure.

He'd already regretted his impulse by the time the words were out of his mouth.

She looked around her stark, dusty, unfurnished wreck of a flat and knew it was time — long past time — to go home.

She pulled her cell phone out of her pocket and turned it on.

No bars.

She walked downstairs in her building and out the front door. She'd find a signal then call the airport and change her ticket. It would take every penny she had to pay the fine for changing the departure date, but she'd do it.

As she emerged onto the sidewalk, she remembered she had no car. And she might possibly still be under arrest, beastly hard to keep track. She set out down Main Street for Junior's office. As she passed the mortuary, Mr. Torkel came out onto the street directly in front of her. From the way he stood in her path, she knew he'd seen her coming.

Was he the one?

Maddy prayed for discernment.

A little wisdom, Lord. It's so long past time that I showed just a bit of it.

She walked up to Dolph. "Yes?"

"I have . . ." His pallid skin turned an alarming shade of red, resembling the rounded top of a thermometer under intense heat. She took a step back in case his head popped. But he grabbed her arm and she tripped over her own two feet, and before she'd caught her balance enough to pull away, he'd taken her straight off the street and into his mortuary.

"Happy Days Are Here Again" warbled in her ears. "Dolph, what are you doing?"

The undertaker was surprisingly strong for a slender, pale man. Of course, vampires were quite strong, if Maddy remembered her vampire lore correctly.

He dragged her straight into the back room, shoved her into a hard wooden chair, and loomed over her, possibly eyeing her neck.

God, protect me.

"All right, you want to know where I was last night? I'll tell you."

The voice — was it him? From his glaring eyes, Maddy had a feeling she was about to find out.

Dolph grabbed her by the shoulders and nearly lifted her out of her chair, anger flashing from his eyes, his cheeks bright red with explosive fury.

Maddy drew in a breath. Scream. Fight. She balled her fists. She'd go down swinging.

"I was in Gillespie . . . rehearsing."

Maddy braced herself to take a swing. Then she realized what he'd said.

"Rehearsing?"

A murder? A kidnapping? You rehearsed such things? Perhaps, if you expected to excel.

"Rehearsing with — my — barbershop quartet." The color in his cheeks faded as if his blood was right now leaking onto the scuzzy carpet.

"You belong to a barbershop quartet?" Maddy's head tilted until her right ear nearly touched her right shoulder, but tipping her brain here and there didn't help. Then the enormity of it hit her. "And you're willing to say so — in front of witnesses?"

"Yes, I do. I'm admitting it right now, out loud. I refuse to live in the shadows any longer. I belong to a barbershop quartet called 'The Four More Ticians.' " Dolph's eyes flashed defiantly. "And we're good. I'm proud of what we're doing. We could go all

299

the way this year."

"All the way to — ?" Transylvania?

"The Cornhusker State Barbershop Quartet Championship."

Maddy averted her mind from Dolph's horrible confession. It was too much to bear. She hoped she didn't end up tarnished simply by coming in here with him.

What else had he said? She knew what a Cornhusker was. She'd lived here for nearly six months now. True, the season was over about the time she'd come, but only a cave-dwelling slug could miss the name of the state's beloved, adored, venerated — okay, worshipped — football team.

Maddy reached for her notebook to consider another direction for her thesis. Perhaps Herbie Husker —

"I hate to talk about it because, well, people can be cruel."

"Well, Dolph, this is a lifestyle you've chosen. Once you admit it, you have to live with the consequences of knowing you'll never be accepted." Maddy's fists were no longer clenched. The fight-or-flight reflex totally disappeared.

Nodding sadly, Dolph now spoke to his toes. "It's almost as bad as when I was a mime in college. I performed for tips in the Gene Lahey Mall in Omaha and ended up in the emergency ward twice."

"You were attacked by muggers? Gang members? Armed robbers?"

"One was a mother with two small children. I got a juice box straw right in the eye. I could have been blinded. Another time an old lady clubbed me over the head with her walker. Twelve stitches and a concussion. There is a very low level of tolerance for mimes and barbershop quartets in this state. Really intolerant."

"Not exclusive to this state, I'd venture to guess."

"I considered suing them for hate crimes, but the laws on the books are completely insufficient. Oh sure, there are protected groups that have hate crime legislation, but not barbershop quartets and mimes, oh no — we're the last group that it's still all right to treat with prejudice. Legalized bigotry is what it is!" Dolph had worked himself up to a rant, but once it was over, he subsided from his anger and his shoulders slumped. "That's why I didn't want to admit it. But since you were in here earlier, I heard that you might suspect me of kidnapping you, dealing drugs, and maybe even killing Melvin Melnik. Well, talk about your Gordian knot."

"Gordon is not what?" Maddy considered

herself bright, but she was lagging far behind Dolph's thought processes.

"It's a terrible, tangled mess, trying to pick the lesser of two evils. Prison or admitting my hobby. Once the word is out, I'll be in another kind of prison, I assure you. But ultimately, I know I have to do the right thing or help a murderer go free, so I have to admit my whereabouts." Dolph glanced up, a dim, pathetic hope glimmering in his eyes. "Is it possible that you could keep the truth from coming out?"

Maddy feared she couldn't make that promise. It was just too juicy. "Not possible, I'm afraid. Junior will have to verify your alibi." And Dora would love it.

Dolph's shoulders sagged, and he nodded in acceptance of what he faced. "Could you give me time? I have to let the others know that I'm going public with their names. They'll need time to prepare."

"I can probably tarry with the news for a few hours. But then, well, this is a murder investigation, Dolph. Once you're cleared, we can focus on other suspects."

"Do what you have to do." Dolph sighed deeply enough to empty air from his toes. "I'll give Junior the names of the other morticians in the group."

The door to Main Street opened, setting

off the happy, happy song. "Hello-o-o-o."

No mistaking that voice. Dora was here.

Dolph looked wildly over Maddy's shoulder to the front of the building. He whispered, his voice desperate. "Please, I've got to make some phone calls before this gets out. Please, just — can you slip out the back door?"

Suddenly Dolph's eyes brightened, and he stood straight, excited, pathetically hopeful. "She's old; maybe she wants to arrange a funeral." Then his excitement changed to panic. "But if she hears this news, she'll go to Jansson's and start talking."

Maddy couldn't quite keep up with the man's emotions. She did respect the extent to which he'd begun to understand Melnik, however.

"Very well, I'll go."

Dora called out again, her voice closer. "Are you here, Adolph?"

"I hate that name. What were my parents thinking?" Dolph grabbed Maddy's arm and dragged her to the back door.

"She may have seen me come in."

"We have to try; it's my only hope." He twisted the doorknob and nearly pitched her outside into the alley that ran behind the Main Street businesses. Then he slammed the door behind her.

Maddy shook her head and decided to walk on toward the police department, although she'd like to see the back of her building. It had been a busy time. She'd yet to fully explore.

But Junior first.

The backs of the buildings were a wreck. Dumpsters, shabby screen doors, and poorly constructed lean-tos. None of the cosmetic efforts on the fronts of the buildings were made back here. Walking quickly, she was near the end of the alley when someone grabbed her and clamped a highly odiferous rag over her mouth and nose.

She didn't even panic or fight. No doubt Dolph had a few more things to discuss. Remain calm.

A harsh whisper reached her ears. "You should have cooperated and disappeared last night."

It was a whisper she recognized immediately.

The chemical smell seemed to muddle her thoughts. Her vision blurred.

Her last thought was that she'd chosen wrongly when she remained calm.

She definitely should have panicked.

20

Feeling slightly panicked, Tyler faced the outlaws.

"Boys, I've got something I need to discuss with you."

He'd found them at the museum.

Carrie had given him an update on Bonnie. No change.

She reassured Tyler there was no need to drive to Gillespie and pace in the hospital waiting room.

He'd taken the boys home, the only place he could feel even slightly hopeful that they'd be able to have an uninterrupted conversation.

Now he faced them. Alone. High noon. Where was Gary Cooper when you needed him? Right now Tyler would even settle for a pacifist Quaker having his back. "Boys, how do you like Maddy?"

"She's great; she talks cool." Ben was fidgeting on the sofa, his tennis shoe twisted up on his lap while he stabbed the sole of it with his shoelace and bounced at the same time.

Johnny cuddled Riley on his lap and took a break from begging to go see Bonnie and asking about the baby. "Can she draw more? Can she draw a picture of our puppy?"

Tyler got up from the chair where he sat across from his sons. Squeezing in between them, he wrapped his arms around their shoulders while they talked about Maddy and puppies and Auntie Bonnie and the baby. This had to be one of the most peaceful moments they'd ever shared. Tyler thought he was finally getting on to being a father.

"I want to ask her to marry me. Would that be okay with you guys?"

Ben shrugged. "Sure, who cares."

"Do I have to give up my room?" Johnny asked.

"No, she'd share mine." Tyler got a little light-headed and decided he'd said enough. The boys might not even notice they had a new mother, since they were never here. But if they did notice, he'd remind them of this talk. And if they didn't like it, and Bonnie was busy with her new baby, then he'd make Maddy handle them.

He changed the subject. "Let's go down

to the swimming pool, okay?"

Tyler loved Melnik's pool. He loved that he could get the boys to the swimming pool by driving just a few blocks, rather than all the way across town like he had in Omaha.

"We swam all the way across the ten-foot end yesterday, Dad." Ben made wild swimming motions with his arms.

Johnny hugged his puppy then set the little golden ball of fur on the floor. "Yep, we don't need you or Aunt Bonnie to come with us anymore."

With a twinge of worry, Tyler said, "I'm going to double-check on that before I say it's okay."

Ben ran for the front door. "I'm walking!" He dashed outside with Johnny hot on his heels.

Tyler's heart hurt a bit. They didn't even need him to drive them. He put the puppy in the backyard and drove quickly to the pool to find out if the boys were being straight with him. He barely beat them to the pool and found out they'd been cleared to go swimming without an adult and could go in the ten-foot end.

The boys moaned in humiliation when he gave them both a hug. Then he went to tell Maddy he'd come up with the perfect way for her to quit worrying about deportation.

She could marry him and move here forever.

Of course he'd said that before, but this time he really meant it.

He'd already padded all the square corners to protect the boys — which meant his home was also Maddy-proof — well, to the extent that was possible.

Tyler checked with Junior at the jail first, not certain where they were with the arrest situation. Junior assured him Maddy was a free woman — for the moment. No paperwork to do, since Junior had never actually gotten around to doing the paperwork to arrest her.

Pulling up to Maddy's building, Tyler realized she could go right ahead with her thesis, as it was, focusing on Maxie, if she'd just write the paper in a favorable light. He'd never ask her to lie, of course, but she could explain this town's interest in Maxie in inspiring words, just as Carrie had. There was no reason to give up her goals and no reason her goals had to hurt Melnik.

In fact, if she did it right, this thesis could be the next in a nice long line of pro-Melnik articles that would help rejuvenate this town.

She didn't answer when he knocked. Since it was a commercial building, he didn't feel like he was trespassing when he tried the door. It was locked. The woman was a fanatic.

He went in through his own unlocked door and went into her place through the adjoining door. She was nowhere to be found.

A niggle of worry crept in as he searched. Someone had kidnapped her last night, but that someone had stolen her car and run. And it was full daylight in Melnik. No one could grab Maddy and take her out of this building without being seen. Of course, he'd have said the same about last night, with a man hiding in her car.

He never should have left her alone. He knew that. Maybe he needed to write it on his hand or something. He kept forgetting his hometown could be dangerous. It just didn't seem real.

Tyler exited Maddy's building through her front door, leaving it unlocked. He looked up and down quiet Main Street. Maybe Carrie had seen her pass the museum.

Tyler passed Maxie, home again in his case, and spoke to Carrie, who was filling in for Bonnie. "Have you seen Maddy?"

"She went by less than an hour ago, Tyler." Carrie came to the door then stopped, eyeing the town mascot. "I'll go see if she's at the grocery store if you'll move Maxie away from the door."

"I thought he was having genetic testing done."

"Me, too. That's why I agreed to cover for Bonnie, but a little bit ago Junior brought him down. He said Marlys at the post office wanted too much to mail him Priority, so he's waiting for the UPS guy to come."

"Why'd you let him leave Maxie?"

"I didn't. But later when I saw the mouse, I called him and yelled at him. He said he'd come by and get him, but he hasn't shown up yet."

"So you've been trapped in here because you were afraid to walk past the mouse?"

"Just shut up and move the stupid thing."

Maxie's official traveling case was nowhere to be seen. Tyler opened the display case and gently settled Maxie into the breast pocket of his polo shirt, adjusting him so he could see out.

Carrie screamed.

Tyler backed away, tucking Maxie out of sight.

Carrie eyed Tyler's pocket with horror. "I wasn't really trapped. If the place had caught fire, I'd definitely have run past Maxie. But I wouldn't have been able to pick him up and save him."

"We need a better sub for the museum."

Tyler pushed aside Maxie's display case, better described as a rectangular aquarium. "Where's Tallulah?"

Carrie stayed well away and kept her eye on Tyler as if he were a potential plague carrier. Which, considering the bubonic plague was spread by vermin, wasn't so far from the truth.

"It's hair day. She's with her sister."

Tyler nodded and headed to Jansson's. What were the chances someone had come and invited Maddy out to lunch? Talk about a plague carrier. Yes, the town had become interested in her since the kidnapping, but she still wasn't exactly popular. Tyler intended to fix that, right after he found her and surrounded her with bubble wrap for the rest of her life.

Dora's huge car was out front of Jansson's. If she didn't know where Maddy was, nobody did.

"Nobody knows where I am." Maddy moaned as she woke up. She was cold.

Ice cold. In pitch darkness.

Her head felt thick. She realized she was on . . . most likely the floor, because she fumbled around and found no edges to the surface on which she lay. She pushed herself to her knees; then, groggy and unsteady,

311

she crawled until she found the wall — chilly metal as far as she could tell — and staggered to her feet.

"Help!" Her voice mocked her, echoing in the strange room.

"Help — someone help me!"

The utter silence was another kind of cold.

Her fuzzy head cleared, the cold air helping her mind focus. Someone had grabbed her. She'd smelled something, a rag. Hard hands. Her brief, hopeless battle in the alley behind the mortuary. Had Torkel followed her out? Did he want his part in the singing group kept silent?

"No, that's stupid." Fear deepened the chill. She felt along the wall until she discovered what must be a door frame. Fumbling, she found a handle. It didn't give.

Locked.

She knew then.

Of course, she'd known all along.

No clumsy fall had tossed her into this room and locked the door behind her.

She'd been kidnapped. Again. What was wrong with this town?

And, unless she was very much mistaken, she'd been thrown into a freezer.

And left.

She started pounding on the door with

the side of her fist.

To die.

She screamed.

Alone.

No, she wasn't alone. She prayed while she pounded and screamed.

In the bitter cold.

Someone had chilled Melvin Melnik's body, too. What other part of Melvin's fate awaited her?

She kept pounding, screaming. Was this room soundproof? Could she be heard by someone on the street? Where was she, anyway? In town, or out in some remote corner of wilderness, in some other meth lab like the one that had exploded last night?

Last night she'd prayed. God had given her an idea and Maxie. Well, no Maxie to help her this time. God would just have to think of something else.

Dear Lord God, give me an idea.

"She went into the undertaker's about an hour ago."

Tyler didn't believe it.

Dora's nose twitched in her excitement to be needed. "I never saw her come past the diner, and if Carrie never saw her come back past the window of the museum, then she must be in there still."

"The mortuary?" But whatever else she was, Dora was no liar. Well, except about everybody's personal hygiene, but even that wasn't lying — she was just mistaken.

Dora nodded until the gray hair on her head stood on end and danced. "And Torkel seemed to be upset about something. They went inside. He had her by the arm. I thought it looked a little funny, so I went in to check. Torkel told me she'd gone out the back."

"They went inside his funeral home?" Torkel was a suspect. Maddy never would have gone in there alone.

"You think he kidnapped her?" Dora jerked in delighted horror. "You think it was him last night?" Then the full impact of the situation hit her. "You think he's the low-down scoundrel who kidnapped Maxie?"

Tyler raced out of the diner. He heard a muted roar of outrage go through Jansson's as the door slammed.

At a flat run, Tyler shoved his way into the mortuary.

"Can I help you?" Torkel emerged from the back room about the time Tyler, still running, reached it.

"Where's Maddy?" Tyler caught Torkel by the lapels of his black suit coat.

Torkel went pale — not that easy for a

guy who was pure white to begin with. "She told you already?"

Tyler only kept from landing a fist in Dolph's face because he didn't want this case thrown out when it was discovered an officer of the court had choked a confession out of the killer.

Tyler roared into the mortician's face. "I asked you where Maddy is. You tell me right now or —"

"She left." Dolph must have detected killing fury in Tyler, which didn't exactly make him psychic. "She's been gone a long time. What happened?"

Tyler lifted the guy onto his toes. "No, she didn't leave. Dora saw her come in here. Carrie never saw her go east on Main Street and Dora never saw her go west past Jansson's. That means she's still here somewhere."

"She went out the back door." Torkel tried to pull Tyler's hands away from his throat.

"Why would she do that?" Shaking the vampire until his un-dead brain rattled, no longer caring about a court case, Tyler leaned down until their noses almost touched.

"Because . . ." A horrible sadness swept over Torkel. Tyler had him. A confession. They'd soon have the truth.

315

"I did it! I did it, all right?"

Tyler tightened his grip on Torkel's coat, and if the guy couldn't breathe, well, too bad. "Tell me what you did."

"I joined a barbershop quartet."

Tyler dropped him, shocked by the enormity of Torkel's confession. "You did what?"

A single tear coursed down Torkel's cheek. "I love it, too. I'm through denying what I am. I'm through with living in the shadows. I'm through being ashamed."

"But where's Maddy?"

"I told her about our group. The Four More Ticians. We're good. We're contenders. But I knew I'd be reviled if word got out. I begged her not to repeat it to anyone. When Dora came into the mortuary, I convinced Maddy to go out the back door so Dora wouldn't start asking questions. You know how she is. Once she knew, the secret would be spread far and wide."

The door sang itself open and Junior came in, backed by Dora and a few dozen other Melnikians.

"She really went out the back door?"

Dora piped up. "She must have, Ty. I came in here pretty soon after Maddy, and she definitely wasn't here, I even went into the back room." Dora arched a gray brow. "Unless he hid her somewhere."

The whole crowd turned to look at the coffins.

"Search the place, top to bottom. Caskets, basement, closets, everywhere. I insist." Torkel clasped his hands together, begging.

The town split up and started opening lids.

Junior stood beside Tyler and they exchanged a glance. It was obvious that Torkel wasn't a bit worried about the search.

"You're telling the truth that she went out the back?"

Torkel nodded. "I'll show you."

Junior called over his shoulder. "Keep searching, all of you. We've got permission, and we're not just taking Torkel's word for it."

Dora peeked around the edge of a lovely light oak casket. "Do you have the lining in anything but white?"

Torkel's eyes lit up until Tyler thought his pupils took on the shape of dollar signs. "You can special order colors, no problem. But it costs more and, honestly, you're lying on top of it; what difference does color make?"

Tyler shook his head as he listened to Torkel try to talk Dora out of spending money. He decided he'd have a talk with Torkel about his sales pitch just as soon as he was sure the guy wasn't a murderer.

"Yeah, but the lid's open."

"I'll be right back to answer all of your questions."

He pointed Tyler and Junior toward the exit door in the back of his suddenly busy store. He didn't go out with them. He abandoned them immediately, obviously hoping to close a few sales.

Before the back door swung shut, Tyler heard Olga Jansson's father yell, "I love a good barbershop quartet."

"Can your group come and sing at our church?" Dora asked.

"You should hear us sing 'Three Blind Mice.' " Torkel's future in Melnik was secure.

Tyler and Junior looked up and down the dingy alley. Then they looked at each other.

"She could be anywhere." Junior pulled out his notebook. "No one watches the alleys in Melnik."

Tyler's eyes went to the west end of the alley, across the street, and right into the window of the post office. "Maybe someone does." He strode in that direction, with Junior huffing to keep up.

Maddy got mad.

She didn't do that very often. She was a

mild-mannered woman and proud of it. Plus, in primary school, if she lost her temper, the children taunted her, saying, "Maddy's mad." Maddy's mad, so she'd learned self-control early. She thought through rather than fought through her problems. There might be a future thesis in that if she survived this ridiculous mouse-infested town.

And since she'd been praying like a woman possessed — possessed by God, so that wasn't so bad — she decided this white-hot fury was the idea God had given her. She began fumbling along the walls of the freezer, or whatever this room was, pounding, kicking, yelling. Her shouts for help didn't qualify as screams anymore. Screaming was weak and cowardly.

She hoped whoever had done this could hear her and would come in to shut her up. She'd just see who came out of that the winner.

Praying with all her soul, yelling with all her might, thinking with all her mind, she circled the room, now realizing it was very small, maybe five by ten feet, no more than seven feet high. There were boxes stacked here and there, and with the room so small, it didn't give her a lot of space to navigate. She came to a wall that didn't feel like smooth metal. Running her hands along it, trying to figure out the rough texture, she realized there was a pattern of grooves. Brick, bitter cold brick. If she was in a freezer, the back wall of it was a room wall. So the freezer wasn't a solid unit.

Shivering, glad for the fury that heated her blood, she ran her hands over the bricks from one side to the other, floor to ceiling. At the top she found a different texture. It might have been her very intelligent brain, but Maddy suspected instead it was her very precious heavenly Father who told her it was a boarded up window.

Could it be that simple? Pull the boards loose, break the glass, climb out?

Maddy's chilled fingers scrambled for purchase along the edges of the board. No loose spots. No place to get a grip. No feeling in her hands.

There was no adjusting to the dark. The human eye had to have a spark of light to function, and there was none in here. She felt for a small box and shoved it up to the window. When she stood on it, her head brushed the ceiling. She fought with the board, barely feeling the scratches on her fingertips and the broken nails.

She stopped and began pounding on the wood. Maybe it would break. Maybe it wasn't as soundproof as the rest of the room seemed to be.

Her whole body began to shudder with cold as she battled on in the dark.

"You're absolutely sure she never came out of that alley in the last hour?"

Tyler stood with his jaw clenched and let Junior ask the questions.

"The street sweeper went by not an hour ago." The postmistress pointed at the wet, tidy street straight across from her. "I love watching the street sweeper, and kids like to follow it. Plus, you know I try to keep an eye on the mailbox in case someone drops in a letter."

They both stared through the back window. It was absolutely true. Marlys Piperson liked to watch.

She was Dora without the spare time.

Add to that, her son was the town terror. He'd been nominated for Boys Town on any number of occasions, but Marlys wouldn't hear of it. Her husband had considered it briefly, even signed the petition that was circulating, but Marlys had rejected the petition outright.

"I did see her come out of the mortuary earlier." Marlys's forehead crinkled. Apparently thinking was painful for her. "She was

321

walking this way. I wondered if she might be bringing a letter to mail. You know she got a letter just the other day. Not enough people write letters anymore. A shame, I tell you. The whole country will be illiterate within ten years at this rate."

"Don't start," Junior snapped. "What happened to Maddy?"

It took guts to speak to Marlys that way. Good thing no one wrote to Junior because Marlys would have held his letters hostage.

Marlys sniffed at the interruption. This was her favorite topic. She'd been postmistress for years, and Tyler, as well as everyone else in town, could move his lips to the "No one writes letters anymore" speech.

"Well, she was just there, and then the street sweeper went by and she wasn't there. How am I supposed to know what happened to her? Maybe she went into Jansson's by the back door."

Even if the whole town wasn't already searching for Maddy, someone would have mentioned such an outrageous etiquette breach.

Marlys, apparently part of some mutant version of a neighborhood watch program, phoned around while they waited. She confirmed that Maddy hadn't been seen leaving the alley from the east end, either.

Her mother lived near the east end and also had a paranoid concern for Jeffie. In fact, Marlys's mother had started the Boys Town petition in hopes of heading off a future prison sentence for her grandson.

Marlys also found someone at Jansson's who agreed to gather a posse, including staking out Maddy's building in case she came home.

Leaving the broader search to Marlys's surprisingly capable network of snoops, Junior and Tyler returned to the alley.

"We'll go door-to-door. We're not going to assume the vacant buildings are really vacant."

The worry was chewing on Tyler's insides. Where was she? How could she disappear?

God, help us find her. Protect her. Please, please, please.

Tyler kept prayers flowing as they entered one building, then another. And found nothing and then more nothing.

Maddy turned her attention from the stubborn window to the boxes.

Who knew what they contained. Maybe a propane heater. Maybe a computer with e-mail access. She could contact a colleague in London and have them phone Melnik to tell Junior she was in distress.

The idea must have come from God, because when she opened the fifth box with her icy fingers, she hit the jackpot.

"This is the last one." Junior emerged from Moonbeam's Antiques shuddering. "I oughta arrest those two just for being weird."

"Yesterday they decided they should have a child." Tyler tried to shake off the smell of incense. "Today they're planning to open a kennel and raise purebred bloodhounds for nonsporting purposes."

"What are they thinking?" Junior growled as they walked to search the final building. "Who's going to buy a bloodhound unless they want to go hunting?"

"It was pretty accommodating of them to let us search their building from top to bottom. But what if whoever took her has another meth lab out in the country? What if they threw her into their car and drove off? We're wasting time going door-to-door." Tyler had Junior by the arm.

Junior shook him off. "Someone would have seen it. Marlys can tell you every car that goes past the post office. Even if she didn't see Maddy, she gave us a rundown on the cars. They were all people she recognized going about their usual business."

Tyler tried the last door. It had been left until last because no one would answer their knocking and it was locked, front and rear. "This has to be it. Where is he?"

"His work takes him out of the building; you know that."

"Well, I'm not waiting." Tyler threw his shoulder into the door and Junior grabbed him.

"If you go in there without permission and we find evidence of a crime, it will be inadmissible. He could get away with murder."

"But if we find Maddy, she can testify. And if we're wrong, then we won't find any evidence."

"It's illegal. We can't go in there without probable cause."

"That stupid *Law & Order.* I'm telling your wife to smash your television."

"We've got five sets. She'll have her work cut out for her."

Tyler turned toward the door. "Probable cause, huh? Like what?"

Junior shrugged. "A corpse visible through the door is always solid."

Tyler clenched his fist. "I'm not waiting until she's dead to save her. That's just stupid. What else?"

"Why are you asking me? You're a lawyer.

You know what probable cause is."

"Yeah, but my brain quit working about an hour ago. Probable cause . . . like a scream?"

A low blast of noise sounded from somewhere deep inside the building.

"What was that?" Junior asked.

It sounded like an air horn to Tyler. "It sounded like a scream to me."

Junior jerked his head in agreement. "I'll testify to that."

Tyler rammed his shoulder into the old, rickety door, and it popped open just as Jamie Bobby Wicksner came charging out of the back room holding a pipe wrench.

Tyler fought his way through the mountain of debris in Wicksner's shop. The air horn sounded again, and this time, Tyler really did think he heard a scream.

From the basement.

Maddy.

Wicksner looked furious. He lifted the wrench. Tyler, desperate to track that blasting horn and the screams, rushed forward, braced for the attack.

Wicksner roared, wielding his wrench, and charged forward two more long steps; then his eyes went wide. He screamed like his hair was on fire, dropped the wrench, and turned to flee.

Tyler dove at the retreating man. He pulled him to the floor amid the garbage strewn all through the building.

Wicksner screamed and fought and — Tyler finally realized — started to cry.

Junior waded into the fray and jerked Wicksner out from under Tyler. "Get away from him. Go see where that screaming is coming from."

Tyler jumped to his feet.

Wicksner's knees buckled and he collapsed. "I'll confess. I killed Melvin, kidnapped the archaeologist, ran a meth lab, kidnapped the archaeologist again, and locked her in my basement freezer. Just please, please get him away from me."

Tyler froze. "I didn't hurt you."

"Not you." Wicksner pointed a trembling finger at Tyler. "Him. It."

Maxie was staring out of Tyler's breast pocket. His little paws seemed to be holding the pocket edge while he snarled at the terrified murderer.

"He touched me! He touched me with that awful mouse. I'm going to have to know a mouse touched me for the rest of my life!" The man grabbed his head and wept. "Please don't let him touch me again. Just take me to jail." Jamie Bobby jerked his head upright. "Are there mice in jail?"

Shaking his head, Junior said, "Nope, we're good."

Jamie Bobby nodded hopelessly and went back to weeping.

"So he confessed to murder because he saw Maxie in your pocket?"

Maddy sat in Junior's office wrapped in a blanket and Tyler's arms. Honestly, this had become her home away from home.

"Yep, a complete *mouse-ko-teer-o-phobe.*" Junior shook his head. Maxie sat proudly on Junior's desk. Another crime solved. A mouse's work was never done. "Tyler handed me Maxie, and I kept Jamie Bobby treed on the soda fountain while Tyler let you out."

"That's musophobe. Really, in a town dedicated to a mouse, you ought to require everyone to commit that word to memory in the fourth grade."

Junior nodded and made a note. "We've found trace evidence in that freezer that proves Melvin was there. And we found another room downstairs Wicksner used to test his furnace equipment; that's where he heated the body. It was all to throw off the time of death and make any alibi harder to break. Wicksner's an alias. Once we ran his prints, we found out he's a hardened criminal, which is why he knew how to conceal his identity and run a meth lab. Melvin knew he'd be let out on bail soon, so Wicksner came and set up shop and waited for his old cellmate to show up. Then the two of them had a fight over money. Wicksner killed him, chilled him, heated him, and stuffed the body in Tyler's building."

"How'd he get a body down Melnik Main Street?"

"The stores all have adjoining basements. And almost all of them are as good as abandoned. He had to get the body out of his own place, and he said Tyler's building was the only one with a cupboard large enough for a body." Junior settled back in his chair and folded his hands, looking so proud of himself Maddy hesitated to remind him that Maxie had solved the crime.

"I knew the basements were down there," Junior added, "but I've never given it much thought. Wicksner could move between his shop and Melvin's without a bit of trouble."

"What about the building that collapsed?" Maddy asked.

"It's not collapsed all the way. I had to climb in the front passenger's side of Dora's car and out the driver's side, but it wasn't a problem." Junior snapped his fingers. "That reminds me — I found Dora's false teeth in her car. I need to tell her they're down there. She was about to go get a new pair."

"Hasn't the car been down there over a year?" Maddy looked between Tyler and Junior. "She's gone without them this long?"

"It's a partial plate and it's not like they're real important teeth. You city people," Junior grumbled. "Always in a hurry."

Tyler shook his head. "All that going on right under our feet. Unbelievable."

Junior produced a business-sized envelope from his desk drawer. "We also got this in the mail today. It was sent to Melvin. Looks like he sent in a follow-up sample of Maxie's fur to that lab. They got back to him today with a confirmation that Maxie is for sure a field mouse."

Tyler did his best to look unconcerned and smug, but Maddy detected an almost overwhelming relief in the man. "Of course he's a field mouse. I never doubted it."

"So Melnik's mascot is safe, then?"

"Yep." Junior scratched away, making notes. "It's all solved."

"Well, good. About time. If you're done questioning Maddy, I'd like some time alone with her, please."

Junior looked up from his notepad. His eyes shifted between Maddy, Tyler, Maxie, and his booklet. Finally, he blinked. "You mean here? You want me to leave?"

"Yes, if you don't mind."

Maddy had to wonder what the man was thinking. "We don't live here, you know."

Tyler's eyebrows gave a startled leap. He supported her as she rose. "Sorry, I forgot."

"You need a ride?" Junior tucked his book away.

"No, we don't need a ride for a block and a half." Maddy said it quickly, because she sensed Tyler was going to say yes.

He escorted her from the police station, not a handcuff in sight. He actually walked with her the whole way home, which should have taken two minutes. Instead, it took an hour and a half.

People wanted to talk about the case.

"Can you come into my office?" Tyler drew her in, holding her hand every step. "I haven't had an update on Bonnie for hours."

A quick call satisfied Tyler about his sister. "Steady progress, but no baby yet."

"Your sister is still in labor?" Maddy winced.

He hung up. "Joe took her over after the first twinge. They're gonna be awhile yet. We can go get the boys and drive over in a few minutes." He took both Maddy's hands.

Uh-oh, he was going to make another

insulting marriage proposal. Maddy wanted to kick herself for how tempted she was to say yes. She'd never imagined the day a man would want to marry her. Any man, let alone one as smart and handsome and decent as Tyler Simpson. And with such excellent coordination.

"I asked you to marry me earlier today, and I want to take that back now."

"No." Maddy refused the proposal before she realized what he'd said. "What?"

"No, you won't let me take that back?" Tyler brightened.

"Wait, I didn't mean to say no. Well, I did mean to say no. I just meant . . ." Maddy shook her head and tried again. "So you want to take it back, then?" She quit talking, decided she'd give him a turn.

"Maddy." Tyler backed up, still holding her hands, drawing her along with him. He sat on the edge of his desk and looked up at her just a bit. It was almost like he was kneeling. "I care about you. I really do. I've had this notion in my head that I need to take care of you. A rescue fantasy, I suppose."

Maddy knit her brow, trying not to outright scowl at the daft man.

He talked faster, obviously not liking what he saw on her face. Wise of him.

"But in case you didn't hear, you're now the lead witness for the prosecution in a murder investigation, and because justice moves slowly in America and you're allowed to stay, you could very possibly be in this country for years. So you no longer need to be rescued."

"I don't have to be rescued from returning to England. You might be surprised to learn I love my country."

Tyler's eyebrows arched. "Honest?" He sounded as if that were unthinkable.

Americans! Maddy did scowl this time. "You were saying?"

"I care about you, Maddy. I made all these excuses to try and keep you and convinced myself I'd be rescuing you, but the truth is, I just don't want you to go. I want time with you, to see if this caring can grow into love."

Well, there was absolutely nothing to scowl about there. "Really?"

Tyler nodded and held her hands more tightly and pulled her closer. "And I think you ought to go ahead and write your Maxie paper as you planned."

"I don't want to hurt this town." Why was the man talking about mice and a doctoral thesis and justice? Maddy wanted him to go back to the "caring can grow into love" part.

"You won't. Once you really do that in-depth study of Melnik, you'll realize that we're a great little town. We are obsessed with Maxie, and while thousands, even millions, might see that as a bad thing, I think on closer examination, you'll come to love Maxie just as we do."

"It's possible. He's saved my life twice."

"See?" Tyler smiled and pulled her closer still. "So your thesis paper will do only good for our town. I'm not even going to give you one bit of input on how to write it. You'll write the truth, and the truth will set us — well, not free, exactly. We're already free, after all. But it'll be good."

Tyler the poet. Maddy would have rolled her eyes if he hadn't held her hands so tightly and kept inching her closer and glancing at her lips. No room for rolled eyes there.

"See if you can change your paper to a more long-term study. I'll do some paperwork that may make it possible for you to get a work visa, especially when they take the trial and your enforced stay in Melnik into consideration, so you won't be poverty-stricken."

"So no financial pressure. No deadline on the paper."

Tyler nodded. "And while you're here, writing and working, we can really get to know each other."

She already knew him. But giving her time was the deepest indication so far of what a fine, decent man he was.

"You can spend time with my boys and see if you have a mother's heart to give them."

The wait would be more for the boys than for her or Tyler.

"We can pray together about whether God has chosen us for each other."

Maddy held his hands more tightly and had to keep her mouth clamped shut to keep from shouting, "I'm ready now!" Honestly, she was glad for the time. She didn't want to marry him for reasons other than love. She wanted to be courted. She wanted to fall in love. Her eyes did some flicking of their own.

Tyler must have been encouraged, because he pulled her those last few inches toward him and kissed her.

After a minute . . . or two . . . Tyler whispered against her lips, "I'm not saying we need a long time."

Maddy laughed and flung her arms around his neck. "All my life I've been clumsy."

"You're not clumsy."

"I beg to differ."

"No, you're just so brilliant. Your mind is always going, and it distracts you from the little things." He slid his arms around her waist and rubbed her back, inching her closer.

Maddy wondered if he was trying to be sneaky. "Like walking?"

"Apparently."

"Well, that is a different spin to put on things. It's quite a theory, that. However much it seems unlikely, I'm going to go ahead and believe it. I've had . . . concerns about children. I might drop a baby right on its little head. I always assumed it was safest not to have them."

"You wouldn't get distracted from a baby." Tyler hugged her tight.

"How long exactly has your sister been in labor, anyway?" It wasn't only dropping them that had Maddy worried.

Tyler laughed. "I think you might forget about the whole rest of the world and only focus on a baby."

"I wouldn't forget about you." She pulled back just enough to meet his eyes. Wonderful eyes. God had made a wonderful dream come true.

"Just to be on the safe side, you can practice being a mom on my boys for a couple of years. They're sturdy. And we can maybe live in a one-story house. No stairs. And carpet every room with really thick, soft . . . uh . . . bouncy carpet. And have wood chips instead of pavement on our sidewalks."

"Sounds wise to me."

"But I think you'd make a wonderful mother."

"You know, considering my . . . um . . . genius-based klutziness, it figures when the time came, I'd fall hard."

"Fall in love?" Tyler's brown eyes sparkled as he pulled her tight against his chest.

Maddy didn't answer. She was much too busy being graceful.

ABOUT THE AUTHOR

Mary Connealy is the author of *Petticoat Ranch, Calico Canyon,* and *Gingham Mountain.* She has recently signed an exclusive contract to write for Barbour Publishing for the next three years. And yes, the ink *was* dry on that contract before she let them see her wacky cozy mysteries.

Mary tells love stories that make people laugh. She lives on a farm in Nebraska with her husband, Ivan. She is the mother of four beautiful daughters: Josie, married to Matt; Wendy; Shelly, married to Aaron; and Katy. Mary's got one granddaughter on the way. And later, if it turns out the doctor was wrong about Josie's baby being a girl, they will look back at this bio and laugh. And Mary will dedicate the next book to her grandson.

You may correspond with this author by writing:

Mary Connealy
Author Relations
PO Box 721
Uhrichsville, OH 44683

The employees of Thorndike Press hope you have enjoyed this Large Print book. All our Thorndike, Wheeler, and Kennebec Large Print titles are designed for easy reading, and all our books are made to last. Other Thorndike Press Large Print books are available at your library, through selected bookstores, or directly from us.

For information about titles, please call:
(800) 223-1244

or visit our Web site at:
http://gale.cengage.com/thorndike

To share your comments, please write:
Publisher
Thorndike Press
10 Water St., Suite 310
Waterville, ME 04901